# PRIME DIRECTIVE

## DUNCAN P. BRADSHAW

For Debbie

"Two possibilities exist: either we are alone in the universe or we are not. Both are equally terrifying."

– Arthur C. Clarke

# BALTIMORE HIGH SCHOOL VIDEO RECORDING

"Well hello children! I'm Dana Fischerman, and I'm here to talk to you today about the Mars Pathfinder mission, and answer some of your questions which you sent us, all the way from Earth.

Let's start with what we're doing here. Our journey began on May 30, 2021, when all the bits and pieces of the Venturer spaceship were finally assembled in orbit. It took five years to put together, with twenty-four countries supplying parts to help it get made.

People asked 'why are you building it up in space for? Why not build it on Earth?' Well, the simple answer is gravity. In order for a rocket to blast away and leave the Earth's atmosphere, it uses a lot of gas. We need every last drop we can get, to help with the first stage of our rockets.

So if we took off from Earth, by the time we got into space, we'd already have used a heck of a lot up.

Even if we were attached to one of them ol' booster rockets, like the old days, it would mean the spacecraft would have to be smaller, and the mission would get harder.

Once it was put together, and despite the ISS accident a few years ago, which your mommy and daddy might have mentioned, the six of us flew up here and started getting ready.

After we checked it over, we were told that we could set off, on our journey to Mars. The flight time was just over five months, and we spent that time getting to know each other and prepare for life on another planet.

As I said earlier, this mission is called Pathfinder. Our goal is to setup a sort of base camp, and test out a number of science projects and equipment, so that future missions know what to expect.

In many ways, we're just like Columbus. When he set foot on America for the first time, he didn't know what he would find, so tried different things out. That's exactly what we're doing. We'll spend two hundred and thirty days on Mars itself, before we pack up, and head back home.

There are six of us in total, I'm Dana, ha ha, I said that already huh? I'm a geologist, which means that I study all the rocks and soil here, to see if I can find new minerals. If I'm lucky, I might even get to see some of the mountains, or Mons as they're called, up close, I sure hope to get a chance before my time here is done.

We have two pilots, Nikolai Tonev, who is from Russia, he's big and strong, but don't let those muscles fool you kids, he's as gentle as a puppy, and he cooks our dinner most nights. The other pilot is Sabina Kreuz, she's from Germany, and is also our medic. So when people get sick, or have an injury, like Nikolai did when we landed, Sabina is on hand to patch them up and make sure they're okay. It's a long way back to a hospital from here!

Then we have Charles Humphries, he's from Great Britain, and he talks all serious. He's funny. Charles is an engineer, and is responsible for making sure that our modules are working and our equipment is tip-top.

All the way from India, there is Sanjay Gupta, who is our botanist, which means he deals with plants. We took a number of different crops and plants from Earth, to see if we can get them to grow on Mars. Some of his experiments are quite fun, and we've even been able to have some fresh corn on the cob all the way out here.

And last...but not least...there's Mei Qiao Zhang, she's from China. Mei is a biologist, and you have probably heard her name a *lot* since we landed. That's because she's been finding loads of little critters in frozen water and what-not. She's just swell, and I'm so happy for her to have so many nice things said about her.

Okay, well, I have to go soon, I have a couple of rovers, which are robots with wheels on, that go around and pick up rock samples for me. Although Mars is smaller than Earth, it's still very big, and this means that they can do more work than I can on my own. Still not found anything…yet…but I keep looking.

Hopefully any day now.

So, before I go, your teachers sent us a message with some of your questions on. This is my favourite part of these little recordings we do.

Every three days.

So, I'll play a few, and see if I can give you some answers to the questions that you've been itching to ask.

**My mommy says that it's all a big load of boloney and that y'all living in a warehouse in Kentucky. How can you prove to her that you're really on Mars?**

Well, I sure know that we're not in Kentucky, those five months of poker and reading the same books sure were real. I guess when we come home, and we land back on Earth, then your mom will see that we really were there.

**How do you do a poopy?**

Okay…we get asked this question *a lot.*

I'd kinda hoped that by now, someone down there who sends us these questions, would start taking them out.

*Like, starting now.*

But to answer your question, we go in a normal toilet, like you would do in your home. Instead of flushing it away into a sewer though, our waste is separated out. Our pee is recycled into water, and our doody is used as fertiliser for Sanjay's little green fingered experiments.

**If you pointed yourself to Earth and threw a football, how long would it take to arrive? Could you throw me a football? I could then catch it and sell it on eBay to pay for a PlayStation.**

Oh…well, it doesn't quite work that way I'm afraid. If we threw a football from here, it would never arrive on Earth. There are so many things wrong with this, that I-

No.

Aw shucks, we didn't bring a football with us. I'm sorry, I won't be able to try this out, sorry sweetie.

**Is it really made of cheese?**

I think you've confused Mars with the Moon there hun.

Even if I were on the Moon.

Which I'm not.

No celestial body is made of cheese. That's just not possible.

M'okay?

**Can you tell us more about what Mei found? It sounds really exciting that she found Martians.**

Right, let's get this straight.

Mei found tiny little worms, okay? Not boggly eyed green skinned aliens, running around, waiting to be discovered.

Do you know how small these things are she

found?

No?

Well, let's say I had a hundred on the palm of my hand, you would still see squat, that's how darn big they are.

Okay…so I think we're out of time.

Yep, I've just had a little beep on my gauntlet to say that I have to go. Thanks for all your really insightful questions kids, they were just swell.

This is Dana Fischerman, geologist, on *Mars*, signing off."

# CHAPTER ONE

Dana bent down, and put an arm under Rex's belly, "C'mon hun, let's see what you've got for momma," she said with a silly voice, reserved for speaking to babies or animals. Scratching Rex under the snout, she patted his hind, as he was placed on top of a stainless steel workbench.

Rummaging through a tray of tools, she settled on a Phillips screwdriver and waved it playfully at Rex, "Let's have none of your funny business today mister. I'm not in the mood for any of your crap." Dana stuck the screwdriver into the first of the screws and did a fist pump, as they began to unwind without trouble.

From elsewhere in the complex, she heard muffled wooting and high fives being distributed with wilful abandon, Dana scrunched up her forehead and pouted, "Great, they've probably found another speck of dirt which wiggles under the microscope. Woop-de-woop."

Dana finished removing the screws holding the hopper into the back of the collection rover, and patted Rex on the front protrusion, which contained the camera and sensors, "Who's a good boy? Hmm? That's right, you are." With that, she untangled the electric cord, which led to a power socket, and jammed the charger into the revealed port in Rex's chassis.

One of three, six-wheeled programmable rovers, Rex, along with its electronic siblings - Scraps and Patches - was pushed against the wall. A red light pulsed on top of the sensor array, indicating that it was being charged.

"Hey, Dana," the thick Russian accent bellowed from the doorway. "Looks like your pet made mess on floor, make sure you clean it up," with that Nikolai slapped the metal frame and walked off towards the sounds of celebration.

Dana stuck her middle finger up to thin air and walked over to the entrance, where a small pile of rocks lay. Pulling on a pair of thin latex gloves - which seemed to be a never-ending commodity within her flight suit pockets - Dana meticulously picked up each stone in turn, examined it, and placed it into her free hand. Every once in a while, she would tut or shake her head disapprovingly.

Sitting back down on the tall stool in front of the workbench, she brushed the collection of rocks into a pile and pulled the hopper she had just retrieved from Rex closer. She punched in the four digit release code and smiled as the light turned green. Prying her fingers into the release lever, she tried to pull it open, to no avail, "Oh shoot," she cursed, mildly.

She placed the metal container - around the size of a shoebox - between her thighs, and plundered the tool tray again, looking for something of use.

With Nikolai's sarcastic comment still playing in her head, she ruled out the screwdriver and pliers, opting instead for a claw hammer. As she held it aloft, a sly smile crept across her face.

Thoughts of smashing it into the stupid Russian's head and wrenching it open, danced across her mind for an instant, before returning to the mundanity of her mission.

Two hundred and twenty one days, back when they had landed, Dana was overflowing with optimism. Their landing site had been chosen as an optimal distance between a possible liquid source, and a promising geological site. Within a fortnight, it was evident that she had lucked out.

As her biologist colleague, Mei, cooed over tiny wriggling microbes; all the while deciding on what to call them, and the wording of her speech for accepting the Nobel Prize, Dana realised that all she had was a pile of crap.

Where once, she had dreamed of uncovering fossilised remains of long dead creatures, or elements beyond classification, all she had amassed was a pile of bland red rock. It had only one redeeming feature, a pungent smell.

Perhaps ejected from some long extinct volcano, the haul sat in the corner of her compartment, oozing sulphur.

She had gotten used to the smell so quickly, that all of the other members of the expedition teased her remorselessly. One - as yet unverified individual - had even gone to the lengths of changing the surname of her heavy duty space suit from 'FISCHERMAN' to 'STINKERMAN'. For a woman with next to no sense of humour before the expedition had even started, it grated on her.

Every.

Single.

Day.

Digging the hammer into the hopper release, she levered away, her cheeks burning red with exertion, her fingers white from the pressure. After a few aborted efforts; one of which Dana had become convinced she had burst a blood vessel in her face, the catch finally pinged open, ripping off a section of skin from her thumb in the process.

"God dang it," she stuck her thumb in her mouth, the coppery warm blood trickled over her tongue and down her throat.

It tasted good. Mind you, anything tasted good after the best part of two years eating the same bland food. She looked forward to the next crewmembers birthday, along with the promise of beef jerky, making herself dribble in the process.

After she wrapped a plaster around her thumb,

which was now throbbing and warm, she turned her attention to the breached hopper, "Please, let there be something, I don't think I can take another day without something, *anything*."

Her silent prayer went unanswered, as another pile of sterile red rock, stinking of egg, was deposited in front of her. Dana pinched the bridge of her nose with her thumb and forefinger, cursing her choice of geology at college.

"Still no luck Dana?"

The archetypal English upper class accent, informed Dana of her visitors identity, "Charles, hi. No, still nothing but this dang rock. Just once, all I want is…"

As her eyes looked down into the barren pile, a glint of something promised a respite from the months of gloom, "Wait a moment…what is that?"

Charles strode into the room and placed a hand on the workbench, "You've found something? Well this is excellent, this will be a day of double celebrations indeed. Mei found a new strain of bacteria from the new core samples she took last week. But enough about her. So. Wow. Good work. What is it?"

Dana waved her hands, partly out of excitement, but mainly to stifle Charles' bluster, his chirpy optimism was really starting to get on her wick, along with his stupid perfect hair, and his stupid perfect face…

She breathed in, and held it.

*It's fine, he can't help it.*

*It's me.*

*That's all.*

*Let it go.*

*Remember Dana, you're the pebble in the stream.*

"Can I help?" Charles offered, his free hand began to move towards the heap of stone.

Dana intercepted it with a gentle swat, "No. Thank you Charles," she mustered through gritted teeth.

*Pebble in the stream.*

With a new pair of non-blood soaked gloves on, she pulled the light stuck to the end of the telescopic arm in closer, the magnifying glass blowing her hands up to double the size. She flicked the light on, bathing the rock in a yellow glow, something winked from within, "There, d'ya see it?"

Charles nodded enthusiastically, "Yes I bloody do, this is so exciting. I mean, it's always exciting anyway, when you...you know, find some rock. But this...well, it's even more exciting...er. As in more exciting...than normal."

Dana looked at him and pulled her 'I'm not impressed face.'

"I'm sorry," Charles spluttered, running a finger around the inside of his collar, "is it hot in here?"

Turning back to the matter in hand, Dana began to root through the pile, until the small square rock was left. Along two edges, they were perfectly smooth and straight, the other two, were pitted and cracked, but still formed a near perfect square.

The surface was mirrored, as Dana turned it in the

light, it shone like a prism, a locked away rainbow sent a shower of colour onto the desk, they both cooed.

"It's…it's…" Dana stumbled on her words. After turning the shiny stone over, her heart sunk.

"It's a piece of a solar panel," Charles finished, the air of triumph was momentarily punctured. "Look," he said, pointing to writing in the corner, "it's made by-"

"YES, I CAN SEE THAT! THANK YOU VERY MUCH CHARLES."

Charles coughed, "Okay then. Erm. I better get back to the others, everyone is in biology. Come and…you know…come along, when you're done here. With your…you know." He tugged at his collar some more, which he was sure was constricting him, then turned and bumbled off to join the other crew. Sounds of adulation increased.

*Well this is just peachy.*

Taking one last look at the section of solar panel, she hissed in annoyance and flung it across the room.

# CHAPTER TWO

"Dinner is served," Charles said with a showman's bow. With the skill of a silver service waiter, he placed a tray down in front of each of the other crewmembers, who were seated around a rectangular metal table.

Dana, still sulking, sipped on her water, and looked at the offering disdainfully," Didn't we have chicken and broccoli yesterday?"

Her moping was interrupted by a tinging of metal on metal. Mei stood up quickly, as if her posterior had come into contact with a drawing pin, she held her mug in the air, "Today, I found a new microbe, one that had laid dormant, hidden away under the surface of Mars, for thousands of years."

Nikolai, Sanjay, Sabina and Charles burst out in thunderous applause, Dana smiled sweetly and slapped her hands together. Enough to make it look like she was clapping, but without adding to the overall noise, "Congratulations dear," she seethed.

"Do you have a name for it yet?" Sanjay asked, secretly hoping that she would name it after him. He had, after all, been nothing if not encouraging.

Sabina glared at him, "Knock it off, Mei will call it some stupid thing with numbers and hyphens in it, stick to your plants Triffid-boy."

Mei bowed to each in turn and took a swig from her cup, "I've yet to name it, that can wait, and no, it'll be something suitable *Sabina*, isn't that right Dana?"

A brief nod confirmed that she had heard her name.

*Pebble in the stream*

"Charles mentioned today that you made a great discovery," Mei said, sniggering immediately afterwards. Charles' face bloomed red with embarrassment, searching the floor for some unseen pit to claim him whole.

Nikolai stifled his laughter long enough to utter, "What are you going to call it Stinkerman?"

"The Dana panel?" Sabina butted in, before the room erupted into laughter again, Charles still averted his gaze, the hole in the ground ever elusive.

*Pebble in the dang stream.*

Dana smiled as best she could, not wishing to come across as a complete miserable bitch, "Well, yes, I found a section of what I believe was the solar panel to the British Beagle 2 lander which was lost in 2003. Judging from the makers stamp and other details, I think it's rather interesting, *actually*."

Charles stirred, "It jolly well is, it's come quite a distance too, considering the impact site we found a few years back. Probably some kind of storm blew it all the way over here. If you don't mind Dana, I'll include it in my report, crediting you, naturally."

Her demeanour turned to one of graciousness, "Why thank you Charles, that would be appreciated," she felt herself glow from within, Mei sat down, and the group ate their rehydrated meal in relative peace, punctuated only by the Chinese woman mentioning possible names for her newly discovered microbe, none of which were universally lauded.

Particularly by Sanjay.

When they had finished eating, Nikolai began to collect the trays and the other eating paraphernalia, "So, who is doing the recording for the Chicago College tomorrow? I'm not wanting to do another one, not after last time," he warned.

Charles coughed, "Well, we all have to do them old chum. Tell you what, you lot have had quite the day, I'll do it, I don't mind."

Dana nodded, "I think I'm going to finally take my trip to the Galle crater tomorrow."

The others looked at one another, Mei finally spoke, "Are you sure Dana? It's quite a trek, and I will need the Benz tomorrow. I booked it in a fortnight ago. I need it."

"That's fine Mei, I can take the Weeble, it'll be a long day, but I'll still be in radio contact," Dana said.

Charles ummed and ahhed, before finally saying,

"Are you absolutely positive Dana? I mean, it was always going to be a luxury if we got it done, more a task for the Trailblazer expedition next year."

"No, it's fine. I want to Charles. I've been putting it off for so long now, that I should just do it. Besides, it will be nice to have some time doing proper field work. All I do all day long is program the rovers, sift through the trash they bring back and then repair them. I *need* this. Okay?" Dana glared at them all, one by one, daring them to disagree.

Sabina held her hands in the air, "You do what you want, I'm planning on running a test fire of the boosters tomorrow, make sure we can still leave this place on time."

"I think it's really good," Mei added, "I feel I've been hogging all of the mission time with my silly experiments."

"Nonsense," Dana replied, waving her away.

*Damn straight you have, you little bitch, 'look at me I found some single celled organism in this puddle of sludge'. Yeah, you look at me like that, I deserve something from this, else I'll just be like…dang, who was he? Not Neil, not Buzz…who the heck was it?*

"I have taken Weeble out about same distance," Nikolai said brusquely, "you'll be fine, just remember the spare battery, I left it in the lander module after last time. And…the…accident. With the sealing lubricant," he added quietly.

Dana raised a manicured eyebrow at him, "Of course, I'll make sure it's securely packed away."

*We all know you were jerking off you psycho.*

"I just need to run you through the procedures for the Weeble. You know. For health and safety reasons. Wouldn't want something to happen to you out there," Charles fussed.

"Fine," Dana simpered, "I'll head out first thing."

Sanjay leant in, "Hey, if you find anything, don't forget your ole pal here. All I've got is my flora and fauna, nothing growing on this rock."

Dana forced a smile and nodded. Nikolai stooped to head into the food storage section, he turned back, "Mind you Dana, at least if you break solar panel, you have spare piece now," his booming laugh carried through, even as he tidied away.

*Pebble in the fucking stream Dana.*

# CHAPTER THREE

DING

The champagne cork ricocheted off the thin metal ceiling and bounced behind a stack of metal crates. "Oops," Mei sniggered, before picking up the first flute, filling it to the brim, and passing it to Charles.

"Don't mind if I do," he said smugly, holding the glass up to the light and studying it intently, "looks like a good vintage."

Dana smiled as sweetly as her bubbling vitriol would allow, she was convinced that she had developed an ulcer from it all, and it was on the verge of bursting.

She hoped the end would be swift, and the gastric explosion would at least maim some of her colleagues in the process.

Wishing to appear magnanimous, she fought the internal urge to grab the glass, instead delicately cupping the bowl with her fingers and mumbling a, "Thank you."

Nikolai snatched his glass from Mei and went to down it, before Charles rested a hand on his arm, "Bad form old chap, best wait for the speech first, then the toast. Don't want to have that and nothing to chink with eh?"

The burly Russian sighed, but acquiesced.

After Sanjay and Sabina were given their glasses, Mei rested the bottle on the table and held her glass aloft, "Well, what can I say? Another day, another discovery, I really am overwhelmed by the sheer amount of raw material available to me here; this will set me up for life. This new bacteria in particular, is far beyond anything that is found on Earth. Just think that this could be millions of years old, waiting for little me to find it," Mei started to well up.

Charles, not wishing to have to deal with female emotions stepped forwards with glass raised, "To Mei, and her amazing discoveries, cheers!"

Five glasses came together and chinked dully, followed by five stunned faces looking at the missing reveller, "What?" Dana asked gruffly, "Oh right." She brought her glass up and crashed into the collection of safety glass champagne flutes held in the air, causing a rogue wave of champagne to splash over Mei's face.

"My eyes," she screamed.

Dana shrugged, "What? It was an accident. Honest. My hand must've slipped."

"Of course it was Dana, and I have grown a pair of testicles in the night," Sabina snapped.

Dana glowered at her, "Well, it would match your manly voice then, wouldn't it."

Holding her face theatrically, Mei whimpered, "Why did you do that Dana?"

The men shot Dana dirty looks, Nikolai's more out of the spilt alcohol, Sanjay for not having the accident named after him, and Charles for the creation of an uncomfortable social setting.

Mei turned around and rooted around the test tube rack, after finally finding what she was after, she held a half full vial of green, gently bubbling liquid in front of Dana's face, "Why are you so jealous of me Dana? We're all in this together. I thought you'd be happy for me, I've found life on another planet."

Unable to contain her rage any longer, she slammed the champagne flute on the table, causing the steam to snap and shatter. "I couldn't give a tiny rat's ass about you finding some old snot in the ground you stupid bitch. It's your attitude, 'oh look at me, I got a chemistry set for Christmas and now I'm credited with finding life outside of Earth'. Like I care. It's not even real life, it's a single cell organism, though I admit, it probably does dwarf your brain huh?"

Mei's bottom lip began to wobble, "I was going to call it Dana."

"What about me?" Sanjay complained.

"Oh for Pete's sake," Dana grumbled. She snatched the test tube from Mei's feeble grip and smashed it against her face, "there, Dana the tube snot, meet Mei, I'm sure you'll be very happy together."

This set Mei off into a flood of tears, her hand held her cheek, as a thin bead of blood formed between her fingers and dropped onto the floor. Sabina slung an arm around her, trying to calm her down.

Charles was busying himself already, cleaning up Dana's broken glass, he rolled his eyes as shards of test tube hit the floor. Nikolai balled his fists, "You are stupid lady, if we were back home, I would teach you lesson."

As they argued, Mei took her hand away from her face. It had started to tingle, a rather pleasant sensation swarmed her skin, it was like someone was tickling her with a feather, she giggled. The other three all looked at her, their faces dropped in unison.

The small cut, which still had a chunk of glass sticking out of it, was fizzing and bubbling. Skin either side of the wound started to blister, burst and drip off, as it did so, it left charred blackened flesh underneath.

As her face sloughed off the bone, leaving a tight black mask of necrotic flesh, Mei laughed uncontrollably. Right until her head snapped off at the neck, hit the floor and shattered into a thousand basalt pieces, all shiny and sharp.

Charles tutted disapprovingly, "Look at what you've done Dana! I'm going to need to get a bigger dustpan and brush now."

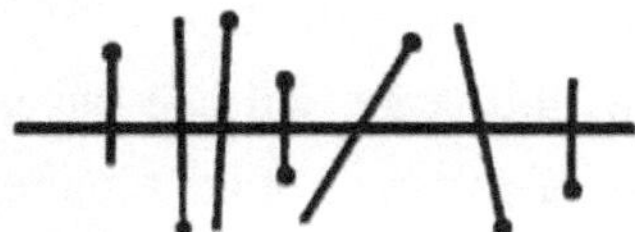

"…ana…"

"...me in Dana…"

"DANA!" the irate tinny electronic voice demanded, with an air of finality.

Dana stirred from her daydream and thumbed the intercom button on her gauntlet cuff, "Sorry, this is Dana. Receiving. Over."

A squall of static buzzed in her ear, "What is your ETA? Over," Charles enquired, with a touch more affability.

Peering into the distance, Dana couldn't make much out except the barren red rock spread out like a giant picnic rug, "I'd guess another hour or so, will contact you when I get there. Over."

"Excellent," Charles chirruped, "we've had some more great news here. Mei and Nikolai were over at Prospectors Basin, and she seems to think that she's found an-"

Dana jabbed another button on her gauntlet, cutting off the audio instantly, "Well isn't that just peachy? Little Miss Perfect has found some more stoopid amoeba. Swell."

Eager to get to her destination, she lent further forwards on the Weeble. Its proper title, was the Personal Single Wheel Transport Unit, but due to a lack of suitable acronym - PSWTU just didn't roll off the tongue - the crew called it a Weeble, after the children's toy with a large ball like base. Even the evil machinations of a most violent  quake, or child, the toy would right itself, much to the infant's chagrin.

With a solar powered dynamo, and the aid of Mars gravity, it managed to motor, and was ideal if you wanted to get around the planets' surface quickly.

This, Dana decided, was exactly what she needed.

Space.

The past seven and a half months on this rock, had gone from being a slight frustration to something akin to a personal affront. Dana laughed to herself, back in training, she and Mei had been thick as thieves, friends even. They were both ultimately selected due to their friendship and synergy of skills. The two of them were there for one thing only, to bring back definitive proof of life on Mars.

It had to be visible, tactile, it needed a name and some quirk which set it apart from anything on Earth. With all the money spent on the Venturer programme, it needed a PR victory.

For Mei, it had arrived within the first week.

That initial discovery was easy for Dana to smile and congratulate her friend on. The video they sent back across the stars was one of united jubilation. They had done it. Anything else that came along now would be a bonus.

Dana didn't mind back then. People, she argued, don't care too much for microscopic things that floated and wriggled around in some kind of gross fluid. They want something tangible, something on the front of a glossy magazine, waving to the earthlings; 'Look at me ma, they saved me from that horrible planet, and now I'm here, selling aftershave and lunchboxes.'

Let her have her moment in the sun, Dana thought, I'll get mine, and when I'll do, they'll be begging me to put it in the Smithsonian.

The inevitable book deals, movie rights and scientific papers lauding her, would come rolling in. She would fall asleep at night, thinking that Sigourney Weaver would be an excellent actress to play her in the inevitable biopic.

Yet, here she was, rumbling around on the desolate surface, with the only thing to show for her troubles being a pile of egg smelling rock, stinking the complex out.

This was her final gambit, the last chance saloon, after this, the only person playing her in a film would be some aging star, that no-one could ever remember the name to. She'd be there, just to make it historically accurate, not to add anything of any relevance.

No.

This was not to be Dana Fischerman's legacy; she had fought off too many lecherous men, eager to get into her underpants, to get to where she was now.

The Galle crater was just over a hundred kilometres from their base camp. It was a geological site of great importance, the aerial shots had shown that, aside from being notorious with its smiley face.

The departure clock was ticking, she knew that to have Sigourney on board, instead of Sig-*who*-ney, it depended on Dana grabbing fate by the balls and tugging it till it bloody well did what it was told.

Much like what she had to do with her long-suffering husband.

It was a risk though. A couple of hours journey there, with an hour, maybe two at best, at the other end. If this failed, that was it.

Ignominy was all she could hope for.

# CHAPTER FOUR

Dana slowed the Weeble down to a crawl as the depression in the rock loomed large. The edge puckered up like skin, after a scab had been picked off. The sun hung over the horizon, offering a tantalising glimpse of the crater.

She brought the vehicle to a standstill and took a moment to take it all in. It was the first time she had been truly alone since they had left Earth. She struggled to remember what the last occasion was. She was sure it involved an awful movie, no doubt her dog Samson, seeking comfort, had sat on her lap, obliviously squashing her and rendering trying to watch anything a moot point.

She smiled to herself. As much as she hated to admit it, she missed home. Dana had spent so long fighting for this opportunity, that life had kinda just passed by. Friends had gone, family relegated to spurned Thanksgiving invitations and hastily scribbled Christmas cards. All sacrificed upon the altar of a chance, of being one of the first people to set foot on another planet. To follow in the footsteps of Cook, Columbus and Magellan.

Sure, she was experiencing…difficulties, but all she needed was one stroke of luck. One piece of good fortune. Dana was convinced, once it presented itself, she'd grab it with both hands. They'd remember *her* name.

With the stresses and strains of the day taking its toll, she checked her air supply, to make sure she was doing okay. *Hmmm, less than I was hoping for, might only get an hour or so.*

As the first strain of doubt surfaced, her intercom crackled and fizzed. Hyper-alert, Dana looked down at the display on her gauntlet.

Odd.

The intercom was still muted. She'd pulsed the all-clear signal via the automatic relay switch when she had arrived; not wishing to speak to any of her colleagues. No doubt Mei had made another amazing discovery of some amorphous jiggling dust particle.

*It's nothing, probably just feedback.*

She turned the engine off, the sprawling mountain ranges of Montana grew in her mind's eye, she allowed herself a wry smile, as Samson pounded past her, chasing a hare into tall grass.

*Dumbass dog.*

"..JFS HGOS DLLDGH HSR…"

Dana tapped her helmet, "Hello? Hello? This is

Dana Fischerman, geologist with the Venturer Pathfinder mission. Do you copy?"

Nothing but the soft humming from the electrical equipment. Annoyed with herself, she jumped off and landed on the red ground, a puff of dust clouded her feet from the impact. The crater ran off in front of her, swamping her view.

The aerial shots which she had studied countless times, failed to do it justice. Now, stood on its precipice, she was reminded of why she had gone to college. This was what it was all about, she was the first person to set foot here, though her time was limited, she was determined to make the most of it.

*Time to make some proper hist-*

"...Dana Fischerman..."

"Huh?" Dana mumbled groggily.

"...you copy?

Dana pressed her intercom button, "Listen, I don't know who this is, but stay off this channel. I'm not in the mood for your jokes, d'ya hear me?"

The intercom clicked off as she released the button, "Should just eject them into space. Useless S.O.B.'s," she murmured to herself.

Stooping down, she quickly dismissed the rubble around her feet as the same boring fodder she had been looking at since they landed. Where once it held promise and allure, now it brought nothing but irritation.

Tottering to the edge, she saw that the crater floor

was just about visible, a gentle slope gave way to a deep basin. Piles of rock cast shadows over the distant floor, which bore a similar hue to the ground she stood on up top. Something seemed odd about the lip though; she knelt down and saw what looked like scorch marks still visible on the surface.

With a tap of her hammer, she chipped a chunk off and turned it over in her hands. It did look as though the side facing up was burned, the rock beneath was the same colour as the floor. It told her little though, she could study it when she got back, perhaps this was an old caldera. It had long been supposed that this area used to be a volcano, or at least had been laid waste to by one.

As she kicked pebbles into the massive hollow, she saw a block of stone further along the edge. Whilst the piles of rock below and scattered around the surface were higgledy piggledy arrangements, this seemed completely different. It looked like it had been quarried.

Dana felt her heart skip a beat, before the sensible voice, and the world weary one, told her to cool her spurs. Each and every time she had gotten her hopes up on this trip, they had been cruelly dashed. Yet, with no other discernible features close by, it was as good a place to start as any.

The closer she got to it, the more certain she was that it was not a natural occurrence. Sides were rounded, and near smooth. At the bottom and top, it looked like bevels and edges had been carved into the rock, forming a squat, dare she say it aloud, Grecian column. When at last she stood before it, her hopes were matched by reality.

Standing around eight foot tall, and formed from the stink-rock, it did indeed look like a cylindrical, man-made column. She ran a brush over the surface facing her, clinging to the notion that she would find names carved upon it. Although there did appear to be characters, it was nothing identifiable, perhaps a fracture that had been blasted smooth by a ferocious storm.

Dana sighed, "Shoot, I was hoping you'd be something." As she looked over the top to stare at the sun which cast a red glow, she noticed something, two protrusions jutting up.

With a foot on the bottom of the stone plinth, she hauled herself up, managing to cling on to the summit with the tips of her fingers. A herculean effort pulled her slowly upwards, as her helmet crested, she stared wide eyed at what was there.

Her surprise almost made her fall off, and she scrabbled around, trying to maintain her grip on the column with both hands and feet. After finally holding on, she once again hauled herself to the top, this time prepared for the sight that awaited her.

Panting, she stood on top of the block, she checked her oxygen and saw that it had knocked off more than she had hoped for, time was of the essence. Carefully, she knelt down, and brushed away the dust which coated the surface, "Ha, jeez, would you look at that?" As the dust swirled in the air, she ran her hand over her find.

Two stone feet.

Both were snapped off at the ankle, but it was clearly a shoe or boot of some kind, as she could just make out detail on top of the foot, and where trousers hung, curving around a Cuban heel.

Her mind swam with the possibilities. Placing a hand next to them, she judged that it was roughly a size ten. The feet stood proudly, pointing away from the crater, over towards the Charitum Montes mountain range, to the south west.

With her game head back on, Dana pulled out the camera from her bag, and started taking pictures from multiple angles. With space a premium, she worked slowly, but methodically, not wanting to fall arse over tit.

After taking a myriad of photos, including a thumbs up selfie, she sat on her haunches, glowing with pride, "Well, I'll be damned. Looks like there was some kind of civilisation here, and who found proof?"

She looked around, nothing and no-one was watching her, Dana chuckled, "Oh yeah, that's right. ME. The hick girl from Montana who y'all thought wouldn't make anything of her life. Well looky here world. After these go out, everyone will know my name."

She swung her legs, as she sat on top of the plinth, enjoying the odd sensation the gravity provided. An idea came to her, and she turned around, and worked her way, so that she was facing out, over the vastness of the Galle crater.

Waiting for the light to quit messing around, she took an array of images from the top of her new discovery. As she looked back at the pictures on the display, revelling in the difference between light and shade, something caught her eye.

Her head moved from the zoomed in image, to the edge of the crater, mere feet away from where she sat. Dana could feel her heart skip a beat in her throat. Shoving the camera back into the pouch on her belt, she worked her way from the edge of the stone block. Carefully, she pushed herself off, and landed on the dusty surface, sending up a small cloud of grit and debris into the air.

As it settled back to the ground, she hopped to the craters lip, barely believing it to be true. Kneeling down, she put her hand out, and ran it over a metal plate, about the same size as a welcome mat.

Daring to look down into the yawning abyss of the crater, she could make out further metal steps, embedded into the wall. A cracked metal bannister ran down the rock, disappearing into the gloom.

# CHAPTER FIVE

Having bounded back to the Weeble, Dana pulled a rope taut around the stone block, and checked to make sure it was secure. Seeing that it held, she walked back to the crater's edge and took a deep breath in.

With her nerves steadied, she took a step from solid ground, onto the metal platform. Despite a number of sphincter clenching creaks, it held. Cautiously, Dana began to descend down the decrepit stairway.

A number of times, she thought she was going to be pitched over the side. With no guard rail between her and a fall, albeit a stunted one with the rope, Dana was still tense.

The stairs ended at another sheet of metal, this time, it ran on into the distance. Even with the light from her suit shining ahead of her, it barely sliced through the gloom.

After waving the rope, to make sure it hadn't

gotten caught on anything, Dana began to edge her way along this newly discovered ledge. The rail bolted to the wall was at least intact, and despite it having come out of its moorings a little, it still felt solid enough when she grabbed hold of it.

Dana craned her head up, and saw that she had come further down the vertical rock face than she had thought. Stars, like twinkling gemstones on a velvet cloth, shimmered above her.

Somehow, seeing them, calmed her down, made her feel that this was just another field trip, that there was nothing to worry about. Okay, so she'd just found the remnants of a bipedal statue, and was traversing down an ancient, near collapsed walkway, but hey, at least she was out doing something.

For too long, she had been the missions grouch, sniping at anyone and everyone who said anything even remotely in praise of Mei. She could feel her confidence return, with renewed vigour, she continued onwards.

Ahead, she saw a dark alcove, sat in the midst of the rock. Creeping forward, she saw the handrail curve around, through a rectangular archway hewn into the wall.

Leaving the rickety walkway, she stood on solid ground once more, her light danced over the smooth passage. Disturbed motes of dust and sand fell lazily around her, glittering in the torchlight. Dana held her hand out, as if it were the first snow of winter.

Taking one last look behind her, at the yawning

chasm of inky blackness, bordering the sparkly sky, Dana held onto the rail, and walked into the unknown.

The first thing that struck her, was the eerie silence, she thought it an obvious thing at first, after all, she hadn't spoken to anyone in some time. But this felt different. She felt utterly isolated, as if she were the sole human left in all of existence. For a brief moment, the thought troubled her, scratching against the inside of her mind.

Memories of the life she had left behind, quite willingly, washed over her. Floods of hugely contrasting emotions sloshed around her psyche, as she plodded down the dark corridor.

Dana thought back to her early twenties, when she had gone on a trip to the Chiquibul cave system in Belize. Having decided that it wasn't exciting enough, she had gone 'off piste' in the hope of finding something of note.

Having wormed her way through a zig-zag section, she saw that the way ahead was impassable. As she was suspended there, between two slabs of rock, she remembered looking forward, to the place her body could not reach.

Feeling the cold rock against her skin, she stared into the darkness, formed after the ring of light afforded to her from her head torch. She felt annoyed, constrained, that her need to explore was hampered by something out of her control.

For if she could just be smaller, or like a gas, then

she could go where no person had ever gone. Find things that no one had ever seen. Frustrated, she finally decided to turn around and head back.

When she was in her sleeping bag that night, thinking back to that moment in time, she realised that she should've been frightened. What if there had been a rockfall, or she had slipped and injured herself?

No one would've known where she was, she would've lay there, stricken, holding onto a glimmer of hope, as it, like her light, faded, and she was left alone, in the dark.

She shook her head, now was not the time to lose focus, she had wanted this moment all her life, and now, her body would not let her down.

As if it were a reminder, Dana looked down to her gauntlet, and tapped the screen. Cursing, she noticed that her air supply had gone down more than she had hoped for. The exertions of getting here had taken out a chunk from her oxygen reserves. At a guess, she would have another twenty minutes, tops, before she would have to turn around and head back.

Just like that cave. The unknown lay before her, and yet again, she would have to turn back, denied by the own limits of her body, "Shut it Dana. Focus."

Trying to rid herself of the negativity, she continued down the tunnel.

"Dana."

Dana gasped, her visor fogged up at the bottom. Nervously, she looked around, trying to work which of her so called colleagues had snuck up on her, to steal her thunder.

Nothing.

The entrance was barely visible, marked only by a wan corona. Tapping her helmet, she turned back to the front, and continued to walk.

*Must be hearing things, probably too excited.*

"Dana?

Can you hear me?

On autopilot, she stammered, "Yes…" before her assertiveness training kicked in, she coughed once, before adding, "Who is this? I must warn you now, I am armed."

"Do not be alarmed Dana.

I mean you no ill intention.

In fact, it is nice to talk to you.

It has been a great deal of time since I have had someone to converse with."

Dana erred, "Okay…I'll bite, how long has it been?"

"Approximate calculations are around one hundred and six thousand, one hundred and ninety two Solus Four years."

"What?" Dana asked incredulously.

"Sorry, I will be more specific.

Two months, one week, six days, fourteen hours and thirty seven minutes.

If my Chronometer is correct.

Considering I have been operating on minimum power this whole time, it is highly likely that I may be a day or two out.

I also have to factor in using your units of time
on an unfamiliar solar cycle.
Please accept my apologies Dana."

"That's…okay?" she replied dumbly. There followed an awkward silence, before Dana piped up, "If you don't mind me asking, what exactly are you?"

"I do not mind you asking at all Dana.
In fact, it is my privilege to have been asked.
Thank you.
I am a survey drone, mapping out solar systems.
This is the seventeenth system I have been to on
my current mission.
Though as you are now aware, I have done little
travelling in some time."

"You don't say," Dana mumbled. She held on to the rail, her head awash with a million thoughts, finally she asked, "So, where are you?"

"I am stationary, in a subterranean chamber
Dana.
Internal diagnostics report that my propulsion
unit is broken, and that a number of ancillary
circuits have been destroyed beyond repair."

"I'm sorry."

"That is okay Dana.
These things are to be expected when you are
caught in the blast radius of a hydrogen bomb
detonation."

"A what? How? Wh-? But if…huh? My head hurts," Dana finally mustered, holding her head in her hands.

"Do you require medical assistance Dana?

I must profess, that I am unable to carry out an emergency trepanation."

"No, no, just…this is all so…."

"What Dana?

"FUCKING HUGE! I mean, a few moments ago, I found some stone feet, probably belonging to some alien statue. Now I'm walking down a hollowed out tunnel, speaking to some kind of Google map robot who got caught in a bomb blast. It's kind of a lot of information to process, you know?" Dana answered.

"I do know Dana."

"Thank you."

"Dana?

"Yes?"

"What is Google map Dana?

"It doesn't matter, look, where are you? Perhaps I can get you out, wait till the folks back at camp see you, I'll be famous," Dana chattered away to herself.

"I fear that you will be unable to locate me in time Dana.

Without a power source, I will not be able to function, or transmit at any level.

My sensors came online when I picked up your radio frequency.

I am quite weak and will expire without assistance."

"Shoot. Well, perhaps I can start, and then head back and get the others? If there were more of us-"

"There are more of you Dana?

"Well, yeah…"

"Interesting.
I would like to study your physiology Dana, I have a supposition as to your origins."

Dana stood, bemused, "Okay…so where are you?"

"I will modify your equipment so that it can locate me Dana.
Please.
There is not much time."

A light, usually reserved for indicating the presence of carbon monoxide began to beep intermittently on Dana's gauntlet. With every step, the beeping would grow faster. "How did you do…no matter, let's go find you."

"Thank you Dana, your assistance is most gratifying."

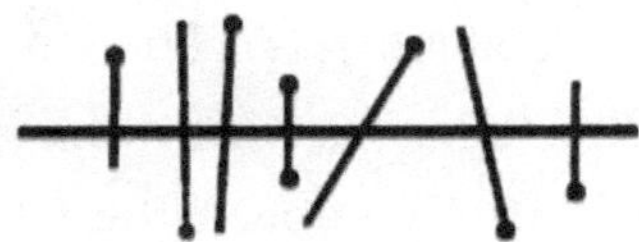

Dana trudged down the corridor, taking a number of twists and turns along the way. Though the beeping grew rapidly, she still hadn't come across any rooms or chambers.

She brushed a thin coating of dust from her gauntlet and looked at the oxygen levels, "Oh no, I've been here too long. I won't have enough oxygen to get back. Shit. SHIT. FUCK. This is just typical, I find proof of extra-terrestrial life, and now I'm going to die out here, and Miss Goody Two Shoes will pry it out of my dead fingers and claim it for herself-"

"Dana?

"-and Nikolai will be all like, 'ha stupid American, I bet she tastes good', and start to work out which bit to tuck into first-"

"Dana?

"-but what about me? Why don't you call it Sanjay? He just drives me insane-"

"Dana?

"-whilst Charles is bumbling around like some dumb schmuck, apologising for the lack of air or something. This is just great."

"Dana?

"WHAT IS IT? Can't you tell I'm kinda busy over here?"

"Do you originate from the third planet of this solar system Dana?

"What? Why? Yes, yes, I do, what's that got to do with anything? Have you been there too? Well, guess what, you can go back, and tell my husband that I've spent the savings on a condo in the Hamptons, and there ain't a dime left," she began to laugh hysterically.

"Why don't you take your helmet off Dana?

"Not a chance. I need to work out how to conserve what oxygen I have left. Oh god…I'm going to die."

"I asked you to take your helmet off Dana."

"Are you not listening to me? I'll die; I think I'll

exhaust all hope before killing myself, thank you very much. I've still got a fair bit left in my tank, I just need to find a way-"

"Take your helmet off Dana."

"No, for all I know, you're a voice in my head. Shit. That's it. Hypoxia. You're just a hallucination. Ha, I get it now, you're just a voice in my head," Dana rabbited on.

CLICK

"What was that?" Dana fumbled around the neck joint, between suit and helmet, "You've disconnected the seal, how did y-"

"I asked you to take your helmet off Dana.
You did not comply, so I overrode your suit's sealing system.
Your technology is very primitive."

"Why did-" she began to gasp, the skin on her face pulled tight over her skull, her eyes bulged from their socket, Dana pawed at the helmet lock, trying desperately to re-engage it.

"It's okay Dana."

# CHAPTER SIX

The Benz, as it was affectionately referred to, bounced across the Martian terrain, chugging along at its top speed of twenty miles an hour, "Not too long now," Sabina spoke breathlessly into her comms.

Charles nodded glumly, as he held onto the bar behind the driver's seat, his eyes straining to see into the distance, where the edge of the Galle crater was visible, "I should've checked on her, something wasn't right, and then when we heard her…well…"

"Dana hasn't been right for a while Charles, I think she did this on purpose. Always been determined to make a name for herself, looks like it'll be the first person to die here," Sabina replied.

"That's a little unfair, I don't believe she would do such a thing, she's just been a bit under the weather that's all. I hope we're not too late."

Sabina laughed, the sound rattled around the intercom, "You are an eternal optimist Charles, I'll give you that. We will be very lucky indeed, if we can get to her before her oxygen runs out."

As if on cue, a red light flashed insistently on their gauntlets, both of them looked down at it, whilst Sabina shrugged it off and tried to squeeze the last drops of velocity from the six wheeled rover, Charles offered up a silent prayer.

They'd not heard from Dana at all to say that she was on her way back. Despite a strange one way conversation they heard over the radio, nothing was untoward. Except as the minutes ticked by, both her voice stopped transmitting and the oxygen level warning sensor began beeping.

With everyone back at base camp, Charles and Sabina suited up and headed out as soon as they could, eager to get to the stricken woman before it was too late. Despite his outward indications, Charles had a ball of doubt as big as his fist, in the pit of his stomach. Gnawing away at him.

Why didn't you go earlier Charles?

Why hadn't you checked Charles?

Why have you left me to die out here Charles?

Each question spun around his head as they bobbed over the rocky terrain, each delivered in Dana's snidey voice, the same one she had reserved for Mei.

"Look, over there."

Sabina's words stirred Charles from his internal castigation. He set aside his guilt, for now, and resolved to find Dana, in whatever state she was in. He followed Sabina's pointing finger and saw the

Weeble set up and ready to go, pointing back towards the direction of where they had just come from.

Spinning the Benz around, the pair jumped out and headed over to the chunky machine. Charles checked it over for signs of activity, "It's primed, ready to go," he confirmed.

Sabina appeared from behind the vehicle, "Affirmative, though some of the supplies are missing. Some rope by the looks of it. Hey, look. There are footprints over here, let's see where they go."

In the corner of his eye, Charles saw the red light flash on solidly for five seconds, before fading to black. That was it. Dana would be down to fumes now, they had to work fast.

They both scuttled as fast as they could, tracking the indentations which ran parallel to the lip of the crater itself, Charles looked up and saw a red stone block ahead, "Look, she must've gone to check that out, there's nothing else here."

Arriving at the column, Charles nodded, "Look," he pointed to a length of rope, and more footprints, which led to the edge of the crater before disappearing altogether. "She must've gone looking for something, come on, let's…what are you doing?"

Sabina was stood in awe of the strange stone monolith, she mumbled, "This looks like it's been…sculpted or carved, look at the base."

Joining her, Charles ran thick gloved fingers down a fissure, "At least she found this…you know…before she went. We should catalogue it, make sure that she at least gets the recognition she deserves. It's the least we can do."

Sabina nodded, still transfixed by the stone block. Walking around it, seemed to reveal new detail, nicks and dents formed in a seemingly intentional pattern, almost like an inscription. She leant in closer, trying to reveal the hidden motif.

"Look Sabina, we should retrieve her body at least, give it a proper burial. In a funny way, she'll be part of this planet, something meaningful." Charles couldn't believe it. Despite her craziness, he'd been quite fond of the bolshie American. She was passionate about what she did.

He had heard the stories of what she had gone through, during the selection process, just to get this opportunity. In a way, he admired her for it. In retrospect, he was a shoo in from the beginning. All he had to do, was get in shape to complete the tests and stay healthy, Mummy and Daddy made sure the right strings were pulled, and the appropriate palms greased.

Sabina tore herself away from the worn inscription, which she could not discern, and looked at the tracks. The pair followed them, and the stretched rope, coming to a stop at the edge of the crater.

"What on earth is that?" Charles said, pointing to a buckled sheet of metal, stuck to the side of the crater. It was jutting out into thin air, a few feet down the wall. The rope hung down to it, before snaking down a set of barely serviceable steps.

Sabina peered down, "This is just…"

Charles nodded, "Very much so, looks like the only way is down."

Lowering himself gently onto the platform, Charles tested its strength, before giving a thumbs up, "It should hold us, just make sure you grab hold of the rope, and no bouncing, okay? Else we'll both go."

Not waiting for Sabina to catch up, Charles made his way down the stairs, catching a glimpse of the sheer scale of the crater, which took up one entire side of his vision.

Reaching a flat walkway, he looked back to see that Sabina had nearly caught him up, with the rope still firmly in his grasp, Charles continued onwards.

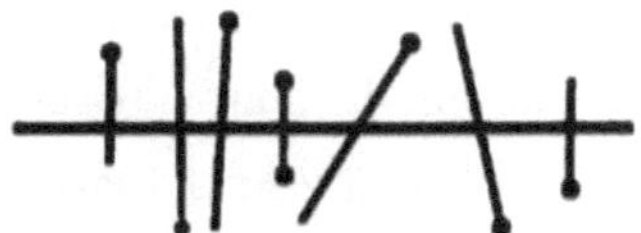

"Wow…" Sabina said, genuinely overawed.

"I know," Charles agreed, standing on the precipice of a dark and dingy tunnel, which ran into the rock itself.

Sabina held up the slack end of the rope, "Well, we know for certain she made it this far, only question is whether she went in *there* or down *there*," she pointed to the bottom of the crater, where rocky outcrops jutted from the gloom.

"Knowing Dana, she went inside, you know what she's like," Charles said. Reluctantly, he turned his suit light on, and crept inside the bowels of the cliff.

Never one for confined spaces, Charles kept his gaze forwards, focussing on the next few steps, rather than the notion that he was making his way deeper into the side of a rock face, on an alien world.

The pair walked on in silence, the only way Charles knew that Sabina was behind him, was with every other step, her light would strobe over the top of his helmet, causing his reflection to appear briefly in his own visor.

They worked their way through the tunnel, before Charles stopped stock still, hand in the air, "Shhh, do you hear that?"

With the thickness of her helmet, Sabina did her best to listen, but couldn't hear anything over her own breathing and the mechanical whirring of her suit, "I can't hear anything?" she hissed back into the intercom.

"It's like…a sort of scraping sound," Charles added, hand cupped to the side of his head, even though it wasn't serving any other purpose apart from appeasing his muscle memory.

Sabina huffed, "Look, there's nothing there, let's just get a move on, we'll have to head back soon, with or without Dana's remains."

Charles nodded, "Quite…let's-"

As he looked forward again, his light ran over a

figure, it made him jolt backwards inside his suit, and he let out a shriek.

Caught in his weak beam of light, Dana emerged from the gloom, with her free hand, she waved.

"It can't be," Sabina mumbled.

Charles, calming himself, called out, "Dana?"

Dana trudged forward, letting go of a length of rope which was pulled taut behind her. Her legs cracked as she stood up to full height. Her head, covered with lank flex-like hair, was still hunkered forwards, leering at the pair ahead of her in the tunnel.

Edging closer, their helmet torches lit her up, the sight took their breath away. Dana looked back, with eyes which jutted out of their sockets, the skin puckered up and held onto the very edge of the eyeball.

Her eyelashes, entwined like the end of exposed wire, were lashed across the white of her eyes, fused together. It gave a maddening, crazy effect, as Dana still tried to blink, but the entire collection of skin and eye merely juddered. A milky residue leaked over the red iris, with a cracked black retina at its centre.

Dana's skin was pulled taut over her skull, like she had been in a wind tunnel too long. Pockets of flesh formed in her cheeks, the excess skin formed jowls around her neck, bursting over the collar of her inner suit.

Teeth were lined with black, as if someone had drawn around each individual peg with a permanent marker. Lips had peeled back and doubled on themselves, exposing the top and bottom of the gums. A fat inflamed tongue slopped out of the back of her throat and tasted the air, through their helmets, they couldn't hear a thing, but they saw Dana mouth, "What?"

Charles reached for her, Dana instinctively flinched, though he persevered. Digging out the earpiece from the folds of skin around her throat, he placed it gently into her ear, which was greeted by a rictus grin. He unmuted the microphone from Dana's gauntlet and nodded at her to continue.

"What?" Dana rasped, now with a lisp.

Sabina and Charles looked at each other, before he managed to reply, "Erm, Dana. Hi. You…erm…seem a little…different?"

Dana looked at her hands, a couple of the glove fingers were ripped, exposing skeletal talons of bone and nail, she shrugged. Unable to contain it, Sabina blurted out, "What the hell is wrong with your face?"

"What do you mean?" Dana replied slowly, prodding her sallow angular features with her fingers.

"You look like someone has smacked you around the back of the head with a shovel, and then tied off the skin like a scarf," Sabina answered.

"It doesn't matter."

"Are you joking? For one, I'm pretty sure you should be dead. Second, you look like an extra from Return of the Living Dead, you're not hungry for brains are you?" Sabina asked, taking another step back. Her hands fumbled over her tool belt, searching for something she could use as a weapon. Pulling out a screwdriver, she decided it was better than nothing.

Dana gave another gum and decayed toothy grin, "I don't care, are you two going to help me with this, or just stand there gawping?"

Charles and Sabina exchanged shrugs, "Help with what Dana? I think we're the ones who will need psychological help when we get back, you look like fucking Skeletor," Sabina wafted the wrench by her side.

Holding up his hands, Charles walked towards Dana, "It's okay Dana, I'm not going to hurt you…"

"I know Charles."

"…what I want you to do, is to tell me. Us. What the bloody hell has happened here. You're out of oxygen, you have no helmet on, Sabina is quite right, you should be dead. And scattered all over this tunnel, in little puddles of goo. Why are you not doing that Dana? Why?" Charles asked.

"I was exploring. Then, I heard a voice. I thought it was in my head first off, but when I said I was running out of oxygen, it told me to take my helmet off."

"And like a crazy lady, you did?" Sabina stated incredulously.

Dana's teeth chattered together, "Of course not silly, I tried to ignore it. But it undid my helmet for me."

"Wait a biscuit dunking moment. This voice, it

*undid* your helmet for you? Does this not strike you as a little…peculiar?" Charles asked, shaking his head.

"Well yes, at first. It felt horrible, like my entire head was going to explode, but then…it sort of got better."

Charles sunk to his knees, "It sort of got better? Dana. You don't look particularly great, y-"

"Better than I should do though eh? Look, the voice told me things, afterwards. I'll tell you later, or maybe *it* can, but we have to work fast. It was down here, but I found it. It told me where it was, only I think it has run out of power now, as it hasn't said anything since I found it. I'm getting worried," Dana, and her boggly eyes stared at her colleagues. "Please."

They peered down the tunnel, behind the cadaverous form of the geologist, and saw a silver tube lay amongst the stark red dust, Dana smiled, pleased with her work, "I've managed to drag it all the way here, it's not too heavy. Will you give me a hand Sabina?"

"I think I will watch over you, if that is okay Dana," Sabina warned, "Charles, help her, if she makes any sudden moves, I'll…you know…" to complete the sentence, she jabbed the screwdriver forwards.

"Fine," Charles sighed, "let's get this done, and get back to base. This is going to make for an interesting report back home."

Dana's face cracked into an approximation of a smile, "One good thing," she drawled, "I won't have to do the video calls to schools anymore."

She looked back at her colleagues, who unanimously agreed with her.

# CHAPTER SEVEN

Nikolai ran his hand over the scratched silver tube, it looked like a large lava lamp, shorn of its spindly legs and completely covered in metal. One end tapered to a dull point, whilst the other opened up to a round port, which was blackened and charred. He looked across to Dana, who, even indoors under normal lighting, looked as though she had been summoned by the Necronomicon.

"Let me get this straight, just so head is clear," Nikolai cracked his knuckles, one by one. "You hear voice in head, saying that it is some kind of probe, which has crash landed on the planet, after a bomb detonation. After it disconnects your helmet seal, leaving you looking like chicken skin from zharkoe, you decide to go and find it?" Dana nodded her head, causing the roll of skin around her neck to wobble. "And then, think it good idea to bring it back here? With us?"

"This is something truly rem-" Dana began to say.

With a raised hand, Nikolai silenced her, "I am not sure how you have not been turned inside out, but I wish to remain looking as I am. I say we get rid of this thing, before it is powered up and decides to turn off air scrubbers." He looked around the dining area, at the rest of the assembled crew. Most were still sat there, in a state of shock and disbelief. Both at the state of Dana, and the strange metal object sat on the table in front of them.

Mei poked it with a pencil, "It does not look like it is active Dana, are you sure you didn't make all of this up?"

Dana ran her swollen tongue over her teeth, the air conditioning drying them out, "Does it look like I made this up?"

"Could just be blind luck," Sanjay interjected, "it is clear that the human physiology is eminently more resilient than we believed. Perhaps you suffered some kind of auditory hallucination, brought on by lack of oxygen. You took your helmet off and somehow survived."

"And that?" Dana pointed at the drone with fingers which were little more than bone covered in skin coloured Clingfilm. Sanjay ummed, and then fell silent.

"Look, all I can tell you is what I have already. There does seem to have been some kind of civilisation on Mars, this drone claimed to have been there when they were annihilated."

"This does not worry you at all?" Nikolai asked.

"Who is to say that this…thing…was not involved, and all you have done is dig it up and bring it into our home."

"I don't think it-" Dana began to speak.

"Enough. All of you," Charles interrupted, having spent the entire time since the trio had returned mulling over everything that occurred. "Look, the simple fact is that we do not know, for certain, what this is," he pointed at the large metal tube. "I think given that, according to Dana at least, it somehow accessed her suit and disconnected her helmet, we have to make sure it is not stored here, with us."

"But, if-"

"Dana, please," Charles said forcefully. "Let me finish. I am not saying that we don't take the remaining few days we have here to study it, of course we do, but it has to be done safely. If it can access the seal-lock on our suits, who knows what else it could interfere with, intentionally or not."

Dana nodded, grudgingly, in agreement, "Fine, but I want to be the one who studies it."

Charles pursed his lips and placed his fingers to them, "For now Dana, we will have to confine you to the medical hab. Everything that has happened, you have to admit, that it's a little strange. We need to run some tests, see what it has done to you."

"You're…you're scared of me?" Dana rasped.

The five crew members looked at Dana nervously, Sanjay looked to the floor, whilst Mei scribbled on the table with her pencil, Charles spoke up, "I wouldn't say scared, just…worried about you. Until you're checked over, you are a potential threat, we need to make sure you're safe. Sabina will run the tests. If you get started now, we should have the results by tomorrow morning. Okay?"

Dana clacked her teeth together, the milky residue pooled in the corner of the dimples where her bulbous eyes met the top of her cheeks. She nodded reluctantly, and the white tears ran off her face onto the floor.

"Nikolai, if you can take this…thing, out to the vehicle hangar, it should be far enough away from us so we don't get any unpleasant surprises," Charles ordered. The Russian nodded and left to go and get suited up.

A ripple of nods and grunts ran around the room, Sabina stood up and looped a hand under Dana's elbow. She went to rebuff it, but it just made Sabina grab tighter, causing Dana to wince. The German woman marched Dana out into the hallway, and headed to the medical bay.

Mei finished scrawling on the table, filled her mug with some tea and also left.

"What do you think is going on here?" Sanjay asked.

Charles sighed, "No idea my friend, a lot of information to take in, within such a short space of time. All we can do is see what the tests come back with, and hope this *thing* is far enough away. I'm sure it'll all blow over Sanjay, but one can't be too careful, eh?"

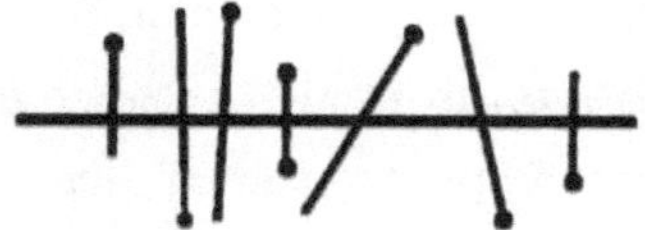

"Okay Dana, if you just relax, this won't take too long at all," Sabina ordered, with her best bedside manner voice.

"You believe me? Don't you? I mean you saw the plinth out there, you saw the tunnel and the drone. You have to believe me?"

Sabina gently pushed Dana back, so that she was lying down on the bed, she raised a finger which warned her patient to shut up and not move. Having gained some order, Sabina began to attach sensors to Dana's arms. Turning the arm over, she saw a chunk taken out of Dana's index finger, "How did you do this?"

"It wanted to find out more about us, so I put my finger in a port, so it could take some blood. My gloves were ruined anyway, figured it would be fine," Dana answered.

Sabina tutted, and went to stick a sensor to Dana's neck. With the thick wodge of skin, she stood there, puzzled. After a few moments of digging amongst the folds of sagging flesh, she managed to place them against some skin which seemed to not pool itself in a gelatinous mass.

With a syringe in hand, Sabina rolled up Dana's sleeve and ran her fingers up and down the arm, trying to locate a vein. The skin was tightly wound around the bone, as if all of the meat, muscle and sinew had just evaporated away, leaving the skeleton intact beneath liver spotted flesh.

Finally, after some coercing, she managed to squeeze a string like vessel towards the surface and jabbed the needle in. Dana went to bite on her lip, but as it was curled over on itself, ended up grinding her teeth together in pain. Flecks of blackened enamel flaked off, lightly dusting her pale blue flight suit.

Sabina pulled the plunger. At first nothing came out, except a swirling mist, as if someone was blowing cigarette smoke out from the hole. There was an audible 'POP', and a thick tar began to pump out into the chamber. After withdrawing half a vials' worth, Sabina plugged the site with a piece of gauze and nodded at Dana to hold it.

Holding it up to the light, the mist hung over the thick viscous liquid like bog gas. The light struggled to penetrate the gloop, and when it did, made a deep purple hue. Sabina shook it, and the goo coated the inside of the syringe chamber, before sliding slowly downwards, leaving the smoke to rise above it.

Sabina walked across to a workbench, and squeezed a drop of the liquid into eight small vials. Sealing each in turn, she arranged them into two rows of four, before placing the samples into a small fridge.

Making her way back to Dana, she noticed she was

staring blankly at the ceiling. Sabina picked up a stethoscope and breathed on the cold metal end to warm it up.

She opened up Dana's top, and placed the end against her sore covered skin, making sure to not burst any of the lesions that dotted her chest. "Well, your heart is still going, though there is a definite arrhythmia, something to keep an eye on at least."

"How did I not die?" Dana asked, still lost in the ceiling staring competition.

Sabina put the stethoscope on the side and picked up a clipboard, jotting down various notes from the cursory examination, "I have absolutely no idea, if I'm being honest. Hopefully we'll find out when these test results come back. How do you feel?"

Dana looked sideways at Sabina, her large eyes stared at her awkwardly, "I feel fine, aside from my face being a little tight. It feels funny to be in here, breathing, like it's wrong somehow? I don't know, can't explain it. The drone seemed to know who we were though, it asked if I was from Earth."

"What happened? You know, when the seal was opened?"

Dana breathed out slowly, a wet rasping noise ran out of her constricted throat and over her inflamed tongue, "It was so quick. First off I was pawing at my face, sure that I was just going to explode. My legs gave way and I rolled around on the ground, I remember tasting the dust, smelling the sulphur, thinking any minute now…I'll be gone, and that bit…I mean Mei, would take all the glory.

Then I realised that it wasn't hurting anymore. I stood up, my eyes hurt, I couldn't close them, but when I tried to move them, they were washed clean, it's weird. Then I heard the voice again, telling me to go and help it. Before it ran out of time."

Sabina wrapped a blood pressure cuff around Dana's arm, and began to pump it up, the words ran around her head. Something jarred, "How did you hear the voice when your helmet and earpiece were out?"

Dana shrugged indifferently, "No idea, guess I must've heard a whisper of it. I just carried on until I found it. Then you and Charles came along and found me."

"You still haven't thanked us yet."

"Why would I? What were you saving me from? I'd have just had to drag it back here on my own. You didn't do anything that I should be thankful for," Dana said.

Sabina scowled, "Are you serious? You nearly died today, we risked ourselves to come and get you."

"But you didn't need to," Dana countered, "I'm fine."

Sabina looked at Dana's contorted features, "Yeah, you look it."

Satisfied that the blood pressure was within acceptable tolerances, Sabina unwound the cuff and started folding the sphygmomanometer away.

"Hello Dana, you have my gratitude."

Dana cocked her head sideways, "Did you hear that?"

Sabina pricked her ears up, but couldn't hear anything except for the background thrumming of the oxygen units, "Nothing there, I-"

Dana sat up bolt upright, "He's awake! We've saved him, I have to go and see him, I have so many questions. Else, when we get home, they'll take him away from me."

Sabina struggled with the woman, who despite her appearance, was strong, "Knock it off Dana, don't make me give you a sedative."

"I need your help Dana.
You have to go back to where you located me.
There is something I require.
Something missing."

A stiff arm clocked Sabina around the side of the head, sending her sprawling to the floor. Dana swivelled on the bed and got up, yanking the sensors from her emaciated form. Shorn of medical devices, she zipped her top up and made her way to the doorway.

As she crossed the threshold into the corridor, she heard a THWIP and felt an icy stab in her shoulder. Dana slapped her hand against the wound as if she had been stung and felt a syringe buried within her body.

The metal wall in front of her began to dissolve and melt away, into a collage of grey and blue lines. She felt light, devoid of form. Sinking to her knees, she managed to see a blurry shape move in front of her. It caught hold of her limp body as she made the descent into unconsciousness.

"I warned you," Sabina whispered, as she laid Dana onto the floor. Rubbing her head, she sized the woman up, opting to drag her by her feet, back to the sanctuary of the bed, where a further dose and restraints awaited.

"You want hand?"

Sabina spun around to see Nikolai walking down the corridor, still in his atmospheric suit, he had his hand shoved under his armpit, she nodded, but looked at him strangely, "What's up with you? I thought you were taking care of the robot thing?"

Nikolai nodded, "I did, it is in hangar. When I was checking it out, I cut my finger on an outlet, thought it was plug socket. Lesson learned, it's not."

Sabina chuckled, "Aww, poor baby cut his 'ickle finger?"

The Russian pulled his hand out and showed her the half inch gash down his index finger which was pouring in blood, "Ouch," she offered, receiving a 'I told you so' look from Nikolai.

"This is why I come to you. Not for sympathy."

Sabina gave him a look, "Good job. C'mon, give me a hand so I can get Gummy here strapped in, then I'll take a look at you."

# CHAPTER EIGHT

Charles sat upright in his bed and stretched, trying to exorcise the grogginess from within. The room swam into view, a dull montage of grey interspersed with garish yellow and black warning signs.

Some mornings, it took a few moments to remember where he was. A planet not of his birth, it gave him goosebumps even now.

Shoving his feet into some slip on shoes, he stood up and made his way over to the sink. His mirrored reflection looked back. After a quick check to see if he needed to shave today or not - and deciding on the latter - he started to brush his teeth.

Thoughts turned to breakfast. He was getting sick to death of porridge; even trying to break the tedium up with the odd freeze dried blueberry or sachet of sweetener, did little to make it taste much better than squidgy crap.

A crafty thought sprung to mind, and he checked his colleague's beds behind him. Sanjay was buried beneath his sheets, snoring gently. The immaculately made bed where Nikolai slept, made him sink.

Though if he was careful…he should be fine. After all, who would be checking? Especially this late into the expedition. They had more than enough food to get them through the remaining time on the surface and the voyage home.

Charles spat out the toothpaste and rinsed the brush, replacing it back into his beaker. He tiptoed out of the module and crept down the corridor. He began to salivate, he hadn't had a slice of the bacon jerky since his birthday, six months ago. Thinking the others would pilfer it before he had some again, he had stashed it away, for just such an occasion.

Everyone was allowed a treat from time to time, surely? And after the day he had endured yesterday, well, Charles convinced himself that he was due something nice for once.

He made his way down the corridor, running his fingers down the shiny metal walls. His mind kept thinking back to the events of the previous day. Did it really happen? How the hell did Dana survive it? His fuzzy head couldn't make head nor tail of it. No matter, bacon fixes all, of that he was sure.

With a cured pig bounce in his step, he rounded the corner, and noticed that the door to the medical bay was ajar. What the hell, he may as well check in on Dana, perhaps some miracle had befallen her overnight and she no longer resembled an avocado stone. He shuddered at the thought of her face, the leathery skin spray painted over every contour of her bone structure.

"Sabina?" he asked, seeing that she was stood with her back to him. She half jumped as she heard her name. Stepping to one side, Charles saw that the bed where Dana had been tethered to, was empty. "Oh god…she's not…well, you know…dead? Is she?"

Sabina shook her head and held up a restraint, the padding had been slashed and the sponge innards exposed like a gutted Ouroboros, "I don't understand how she could've gotten out, I double checked it myself."

Charles walked to the bed, the sheets were coated in a musty looking yellow glaze, making him think of the Turin shroud. Each restraint had been torn apart, no subtlety, or gentle teasing out of the appendage, just plain old brute force, "I don't get it…"

"Neither do I," Sabina replied with an exasperated sigh, "the sedative alone should've knocked her out till this morning. None of this makes sense."

"Could she have had help?" Charles asked, piecing the ragged ends of a leg restraint together.

"Like who? No one in their right mind would help her. If so, why not just unbuckle the strap? You wouldn't have to tear it apart like an animal."

"Not unless you didn't know what you were doing…"

"Conjecture Charles. If she was infected with something, which has made her have voices in her head, then no one else here has gone through what she has, have they?" Sabina asked, looking for an answer.

"Although…"

"What?" Charles asked.

Sabina folded her arms, "She said that she let the *thing* take some of her blood, that can't be good."

Charles put the restraint down and shook his head, "No, I guess not. Anyway, where the hell did she go?" he asked aloud, pondering with his fingers tapping his teeth.

Sabina sagged, "It has to be something to do with that drone thing we found her with yesterday, come on, let's go and check."

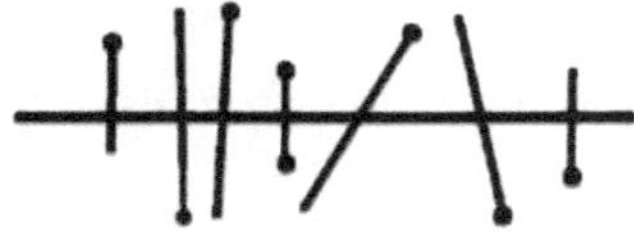

An hour later, the crew were sat around the dining table, a gentle din echoed off the walls, Charles knocked a fork against a metal mug, "Okay everyone, can we have some hush please," he said in his best teacher's voice, "thank you."

Whilst the others remained sitting, sipping on coffee, or chewing on some crackers, Charles rested his hands on the edge of the table, finally he spoke, "The situation is this; at some point during the night, Dana broke free from her restraints in medical and escaped base camp. Not satisfied with this feat of escapology, she has also taken the Benz."

A round of hushed whispers, accusatory jabs and looks ran around the group, Charles raised his hands, "Please, people, one at a time, okay? She has also taken the drone that was found yesterday. Sabina said that she became agitated last night, and that Dana said she heard it talking to her, when there was nothing there. She became aggressive and had to be sedated."

Nikolai shifted in his chair, "Heard voices? Like what?"

"She didn't say, just that 'he was awake', next thing I know she's hit me and tried to leave," Sabina replied, turning her head sideways to show a purple bruise peeking out from her hairline.

"Ouchy," Mei said, "this is very interesting, but what can we do? We don't know where she's gone. For all we know, she might be dead already."

Charles and Sanjay gasped, "What?" Mei said innocently. "We have to include it as a possibility, Dana was hardly the pinnacle of mental stability before she…you know…had the thing happen to her yesterday. Poor woman."

"I have a theory," Sanjay ventured, "perhaps she went back out to the Galle crater? It's the only logical place really, where else has she been to on Mars? Perhaps there is something else out there, trying to talk to her?"

Charles nodded, "It's what we thought too," he thumbed between himself and Sabina, "it's the most likely candidate. Which means that you've just volunteered old chum."

Sanjay's smile fell off his face, "What do you mean? Volunteered? For what?"

Sabina stood up, "She took the Benz, so we need to use the MMUs, the three of us will head out there, see if she did indeed go back. If so, we'll get her, the Benz, and bring them both back here."

"What about us?" Mei asked.

"You and Nikolai stay here. Then if she comes back, there's more than one person here to deal with her," Charles pointed out.

Nikolai nodded, "That is good. I am happy with that, I can carry out diagnostics on the generator, something is not right with it."

"Excellent, all decided then, we best get a move on, it's a bit of a poke out there. Make sure you take your motion sickness pills Sanjay, it's going to be a bit…choppy," Charles said with a cheeky smile.

# CHAPTER NINE

The three astronauts jolted and bobbed across the surface. Their Manned Maneuvering Units were equipped with a small pair of thrusters, originally intended for use in space.

With the Weeble still awaiting recovery and the Benz stolen, it was all they had. A quick burst would send them soaring skywards, before gently sinking. Using this method, they were bunny hopping their way towards the Galle crater.

With their added height, they could make out the distinctive smiley face which made the Galle crater so widely renowned. Every ascension brought it into sight, on the way down, it looked like it was winking at them, beckoning them forwards suggestively.

"Look," Sabina yelled through the intercom, "there's the Benz."

A short way off sat the six wheeled rover, the tyre tracks and skid at the end were visible from their elevated viewpoint.

Each of them brought their bouncing to a halt a few hundred metres from the parked vehicle, wishing to maintain the element of surprise. They trotted the rest of the way as quickly as they could, though the bulk of the MMU did not make the process easy.

Finally arriving, Sanjay headed to the Benz, and began to check it out, "Looks like it's operational to me."

"And she's left the drone in the cargo rack too. This is going to be easy peasy," Charles said confidently.

Sanjay sighed disapprovingly, "You've just jinxed us now, you idiot. Where did you say this tunnel was?"

The trio teetered to the edge of the crater, Charles pointed down to the metal platform, "Wow. Just…wow," Sanjay muttered.

"We need to get down there and find her, we don't have all day. Though someone needs to stay with the Benz, we can't let her steal it again," Sabina said.

Sanjay stuck his hand up, "I'll do it."

Charles looked across, "Are you sure Sanj?"

"If I see Boney M has got around you, and is crawling up those stairs, I'll radio you guys, and floor it. I can keep her busy, whilst you get back up top, I'll pick you up and leave her for dead. We can work out how to snag her together then."

"True," Charles conceded. "Snag her? She's not a salmon you know."

"Plus, it's clear that she's not of the right mind, if

it gets lairy, then I can leave that business to you two. I'm a lover, not a fighter," Sanjay added.

Sabina patted Charles on the shoulder, "Let's go find her."

She went to unhook her MMU, before Charles shook his head, "The lights on these are brighter than our helmet torches, plus, the extra oxygen on board might come in handy."

Taking one last look back at Sanjay, who waved them adieu, Charles and Sabina lowered themselves onto the metal ledge, before working their way towards the tunnel.

# CHAPTER TEN

The twin lights atop the MMU easily cut through the murk and gloom which clogged the tunnel system. Charles had taken the lead, and the extra illumination showed more detail to their surroundings, which they had missed the first time round.

Within the walls were interred thick pipes, which ran in straight lines around waist height. Though there were no doorways or alcoves, there were rusted metal signs affixed to the wall, every few hundred feet. Any symbol or warning had long since been scoured from their surface.

The journey was made in near silence, only when they found some new detail, did one of them venture a word or two. After a myriad of twists and turns, Charles pointed forwards, "Look, there's something up ahead." With a degree of hesitation, they worked their way towards it.

The chunky pipes ended as they hit the wall, disappearing into the room beyond. A large metal door stood before them, slightly ajar. To one side was a panel which had been wrenched free from its housing.

Exposed wires had been pulled apart and wound round each other, Charles went to touch them, but retracted as sparks crackled from the contact points.

With the corridor having opened up to accommodate the wider doorway, Sabina lifted the keypad which was hanging downwards, having been ripped free to allow admittance to the wiry innards.

"Look," she whispered. Sabina held the metal and plastic plate up to Charles, who gasped. There were three columns of off-white square buttons, and four rows, above a metal grille.

Sabina scraped a gloved finger across the buttons, to reveal neatly formed characters beneath. Though some were angular designs of no significance, here and there were shapes formed into numbers. "Is that a seven?" she asked.

Charles cradled the keypad and examined it closer, before nodding his head, "This is most strange indeed, how can this be?"

"We can look at this another time, come on, let's see what is behind door number one," Sabina faced forwards, lighting up the barrier before them.

It was a deep brown, with rust forming vast patches of orange, mainly around the hinges and a rectangular hatch around eye height. Charles let the keypad go, and placed his hands against the bulky door, pushing it open.

Even through their suits, they could hear the sound of metal grinding against stone. Inexorably it opened up to reveal a large stone walled chamber within.

The bulk of their MMU suits stopped them from slipping through until the door had been opened near fully. Finally, panting from exertion, Sabina and Charles staggered through the open door.

"What is this place?" Charles asked. He turned this way and that, allowing the heavy duty lights to blaze over the interior.

Sabina walked off to one side, "Looks like it was used as a storage depot of some kind, all these boxes..." She ran her fingers over dust covered containers, identical sizes, stacked and running from floor to ceiling. Fragile sheaves of paper fluttered from the sides.

Daring to touch one, it fell apart between her fingers, the fragments slowly falling to the floor. Looking down, she saw footprints stamped onto the grime on the floor. As she followed them, she beckoned Charles to follow.

From either side of her vision, the wall of boxes disappeared, and the feeling of claustrophobia dissipated. Seeing the tracks run off in a straight line, Sabina looked up, "My god..."

Charles was a few steps behind, moving around the bulky stationary figure of Sabina, he stumbled to a halt.

Before them were rows of the boxes which were

behind them. They had been arranged neatly either side of an aisle, where the footprints continued down. With the appearance of a church, everything was pointing towards a stone plinth at the end, which was covered in a cloth sheet.

Having found an ounce of resolve, Charles took a deep breath and walked down the aisle. As he did so, he looked from side to side, at the mass of skeletons which were resting in ramshackle piles. The bone collection spilled from the top of the boxes, and onto the floor.

They looked human, and were of all shapes and sizes. One cluster was comprised of a group of four distinct individuals. Amongst the bone cairn, were two small skulls, resting within the ribcages of two larger specimens.

"They're all looking forward," Sabina said, appearing from behind Charles, making him jump a little inside.

Charles nodded, "It's not just that, they all look…so peaceful. None of them are at the doorway, or anywhere else. It's like they sat down, and just died."

"How did they die though? Looks like they've been down here a while, well preserved too by the looks of it," Sabina knelt down, and looked over a thigh bone, morsels of flesh still ran within its fissures.

"With the door, and the panel we found, I'd guess that they were sealed in."

Sabina put the bone down, "But by who…or what?"

Sensing one obvious answer, the pair shared a nervous glance, before Charles pointed to the covered plinth, "Come on, let's go see what they were here for."

As they made their way down the aisle, Charles thought back to Harvest festivals at school. Carrying loaves of bread and canned goods, down to a basket in front of the church altar.

Not quite understanding what they were doing, he remembered looking at the craggy faces of the old folks which had been invited to the service. Some were looking forward, putting up with the idolatry to get some food in return.

Others though, they looked back at him. Their faces, worn and leathered by time, lit up, as they looked at the children, and the promise they had. Both in terms of vitality and the gifts they had brought with them.

The skeletal remains looked back at him that same way, examining the intruders, "This place…it's like a temple or something," he said.

Sabina pushed past him, "This place is no temple. It's a tomb."

As they got to the front, they saw a number of bone piles lined up in an orderly row. An arm reached forwards in death, finger bones touching the bottom of the cloth, which was draped over the makeshift altar.

Charles tried to paw the dust away, to see the surface clearer. The debris was too ingrained, and his work merely left finger marks through the grey, dulled surface.

"Don't worry about that, look," Sabina gestured to the top.

The cloth at the summit of the altar, was resplendent, in red and white lines. An outline of some*thing* created a swathe of colour in the dust and muck. At the edge, before it was reclaimed by the drab dustlands once more, a white star bloomed over a dark blue background.

Taking a step back, Sabina said, "This is where that *thing* was, the drone, which Dana found and took back."

Charles nodded, "Of course." He looked back down the room, at the congregation of bones, "They were worshipping it…this thing, look at them."

For a moment, the pair looked at the ossuary laid out before them, the faithful following to a metal god. "How did it do this to them all? Why kill all these people, when they obviously revered it? It just doesn't make sense." Charles said.

"It doesn't matter, what it is. Dana is under its control, we've got to find her, who knows what it wants her to do?"

"Why did she come back?"

Sabina stepped over the altar, and rummaged through an open box of junk, "I don't know, perhaps there was something missing, something that it needed?"

Charles looked around, "Well, if we didn't pass her on the way, and she's not here now, where did she get to?"

Sabina gulped, and stood up. Looking around frantically, she saw a pair of footprints lead off to the corner of the room, where another metal door, albeit smaller, was swung open, "Oh no, we have to warn Sanjay."

# CHAPTER ELEVEN

Sitting in the driving seat of the Benz, Sanjay pretended to turn the wheel, making vroom sounds, screeching round the imaginary corners of Silverstone.

In his best Murray Walker accent, he commentated, "And it's Sanjay Gupta, in the lead, from Hamilton and Rosberg. A win today, and he'll be confirmed as world champion. What a drive from the lad from Mumbai."

From his left side he heard a cracking sound, like a glass table giving way under pressure from a heavy encyclopaedia. Tearing himself from the fictitious British Grand Prix, and allowing the two Mercedes drivers to overtake him in the process, Sanjay tried to work out where the sound was coming from.

A short distance away, a cloud of dust puffed up from the ground. Sanjay felt a rumble run beneath him. On autopilot, he climbed out of the driver's cabin and stumbled towards the disturbance.

He could feel his heartbeat thumping against the side of his temple. Just as the tremors began to subside, he felt another beneath him. Closer to the epicentre, the sensation overlapped with a cracking sound.

The cloud of dust grew like a ball being pumped up, the outer reaches of its gritty grasp had reached his visor. He could hear tiny flecks of rock hit the Plexiglas.

Trying to find the source of the quake, he bent down and wafted his hand through the miasma, trying to clear enough so that he could see what the cause of his consternation was.

In front of him, the ground shook once more. As it did, pebbles and a sheet of sediment rattled and slid downwards, as a flat metal hatch began to creak open. Sanjay, despite every fibre of his being telling him to run, edged closer, determined to discover the mystery.

The hatch opened to around forty five degrees, before stopping still. Hands, fingers scoured to the bone, appeared either side of the opening. Even through his helmet, he could hear the bone grinding against the rock, trying to gain purchase, "Errr, guys?" he spoke into the intercom, greeted only by static.

"Guys?" he asked again, this time, more desperate.

"Hello Sanjay."

"Who is this?"

"I'm a friend Sanjay.
You can trust me."

"Balls I can, you're the thing that gave Dana her

face job, you ain't getting me," Sanjay ran his fingers around the duct tape he had wound around the seal between suit and helmet, making sure it was stuck fast.

"All I'm doing Sanjay, is completing my prime directive.
I have been rendered inoperable for some time,
I have to finish what I started."

Sanjay began to edge backwards, though he was transfixed by the darkened shaft, "What do you mean? What did you start?"

"The end Sanjay.
I started the end.
Behind you."

Sanjay darted around, staring back at the Benz, "Eh? There's nothing there?"

"How about now Sanjay?

Sanjay turned back, and saw a figure crawling out of the void. As it pulled itself to its full height, he saw Dana's pulled tight face looking back. "How did…?"

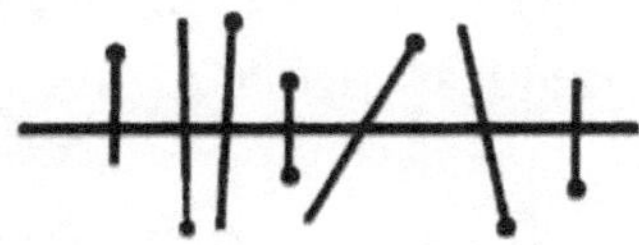

Sanjay's question echoed through the intercom, Dana and Charles looked at each other, "Sanjay! Get out of there now, something's wrong. You need to get back to base. Do you copy?"

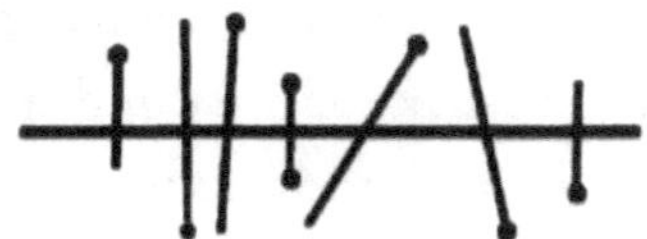



Sanjay shook his head, Dana was bearing down on him, whilst he was stood still like an idiot, "Join you? No way, I'm getting out of here." Adrenalin flooded his system and belatedly, he turned and started to make his way back to the Benz.

It felt like he was wading through a chest high snowdrift. Laboured step was followed by laboured step. He could feel the air being constricted around him.



"Good luck with that," he replied. The Benz was now only a few metres away, he knew that there was no way Dana could catch him. The rules of physics apply to everyone, he deduced, even psychos.

Sanjay clambered into the driving seat, he turned his head sideways to see that she was still some distance away.



Sanjay raised his middle finger to the lumbering figure, "Fuck you nutjob, eat my dust." He heard a click, and then his visor plunged the world into darkness, Sanjay panted heavily, all he could see was his panicked reflection against the blackness of the visor.

He thrashed about, trying to find the ignition, if he could just start the bloody thing, he could get out of there, it wasn't as if he could plough into a bus stop of old age pensioners.

With the thickness of his gloves, his tactility was reduced; it was like trying to pick up an apple with chopsticks. His chubby fingers worked over the dashboard, pressing buttons at random, yearning to hear the sound of the engine grumbling into life and escape being effected.

A sharp pain in his wrists knocked his arms downwards, he heard a clunk as the helmet connected with the steering wheel. Inside, his forehead smacked against the visor, still utterly black.

Shaking his head, Sanjay looked into his own fear-filled eyes. A snail of snot stuck out from the shell of his nose, he could feel a welt growing on his forehead.

Two dull thuds sounded either side of his helmet, around his ears, Sanjay tried to turn, but to no avail. He was then yanked to one side and felt himself in an awkward embrace.

Silence.

Nothing but the womb like feeling of warmth and terror, knowing that soon, the sanctuary called home would be gone, and he'd be pulled into the world, screaming. His head rocked backwards as he felt something thud against the front of his visor.

Another smack prefaced a cracking sound. His reflection splintered into a jigsaw image, separated by a spider web of cracked glass. He was pummelled again, and again, each blow causing the fissures to spread wider, beyond his peripheral vision. A hiss blew air against his chin, and he began to gasp. It felt like someone had secreted a flaccid balloon between his ears, in his nasal cavity and had begun to inflate it.

Then he felt a fist smack him in the nose, as the visor was breached. Light flooded in, bathing him in a red glaze. Sanjay felt the air being pulled from his lungs. Invisible fingers had dug into the skin at the back of his head and twisted, like a corkscrew. With each slow rotation, he could feel his flesh pulled taut over his cracking cheekbones.

Dana's face loomed into view, at such close range, she looked even more grotesque, her hands reaching for him, through the broken visor. Ignoring shards of glass scratching down the tough skin, her thumbs reached out for him, the ends worn away to pointed bone.

Sanjay screamed unbidden as the jagged talons pierced the soft squishy eyeballs and dug into his sockets. Fingers ran under his chin and cheeks, as if holding his skull like a goblet. With the thumbs anchored inside Sanjay's head, the hands squeezed together, and began to crush.

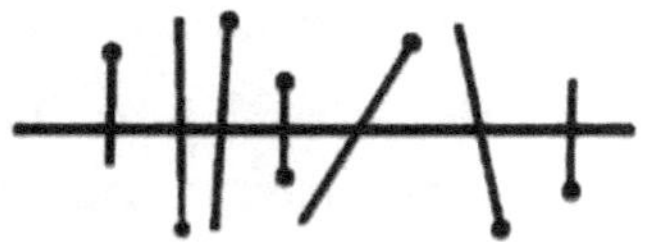

Sabina and Charles had just made it back to the tunnel entrance, when the sound of guttural screaming flooded their ears. Unintelligible words, mingled with whimpering, squelching and cracking was all they could hear. They both fired up their MMU packs and burst over the edge of the crater, a little way off, they saw the Benz parked up.

They both landed and turned towards the rover, a figure pulled Sanjay from the drivers' seat as if he were a mannequin, and cast him aside. In slow motion, the body hung in the air, descending like a feather on a gentle breeze. The Benz spluttered into life and turned violently, heading back in the direction they had just come.

Charles got to Sanjay first, his lifeless body gently landed onto the surface. Placing a hand under the helmet, he dared to look. Through the smashed in visor, he could see the stump of Sanjay's neck. Tendrils of vein and muscle hung limply in the air, nothing else of the head remained. It reminded him of a film he had seen as a kid, where a robot had had his head taken off, leaving wires and sparks in its place.

Sabina stood over the pair, trying not to look at the ruin where Sanjay's head used to be, "What do we do?"

Charles set the body down, "We have to get back to base, now. We have to stop her."

# CHAPTER TWELVE

Mei leaned back on her chair and peered down either side of the corridor. Confident that she was alone, she wheeled across to the desk. Picking up an empty glass beaker, she fixed a toothy smile to her face, "This is such a shock! I thought I was just here to make up the numbers, that there would be no way that I would win. I don't know what to say," she enthused.

Her face turned serious as if a switch had been flicked, "I would like to thank my mum, my dad, and my teacher Mister Ying. Without your guidance and instruction, I would not be here today, claiming such a prestigious award. They say that human life is…"

She shook her head, "No, silly, too fake, need to make it more…natural…got to stay calm…keep it light. This is my chance to show all of them how wrong they were. Pffft, what did they know? I showed them. Me."

A bony finger coiled a ringlet of hair around her ear, Mei replaced the beaker back onto the desk and shook her hands. Another tooth cliff-face smile broke out, "Me? But I-" A clatter of metal hitting the floor outside made her jump, nearly smashing the beaker prize in the process, as her arm swung wildly.

Standing slowly, Mei inched across the floor, to the doorway. Ensconced against the side, she could see that one direction was clear, she couldn't hear anything except the hum of machinery. She gulped, and balled her tiny fists, certain that whatever was out there, she would wallop them.

Reluctantly, she gripped hold of the doorway and eased her head around the corner, not knowing what or who to expect.

Nothing.

A ladder lay across the width of the corridor, still reverberating. "Ha, knew it was nothing."

She sighed gladly, turning so her back was against the wall and holding her chest, hoping it would make it slow down. As it was, she was convinced that her heart could still burst free at any moment.

She smiled at her silliness and went to walk back to her desk, "All fixed," came a thickly accented voice, Mei screamed. With hands affixed to the side of her mouth, as if acting as a loudspeaker, she bolted as fast as she could, deeper into the room. Quickly, she remembered that there was no other exit, and her laboratory was not exactly palatial. Unable to slow down, she smacked head first into a wall, and stood there, dazed.

A booming laugh came from the doorway,

clutching her head, Mei turned around to see Nikolai standing there, creased over in fits of laughter. "Stupid man," she yelled, "you scared me half to death."

Nikolai fought to compose himself, rubbing a tear from his eye, "You should see face. So funny. Only half to death? How would I make it all the way?"

Mei picked up the closest thing to her, a sodden towel, and threw it at Nikolai, who caught it with his face, it did little to shut him up. "It's creepy enough when everyone is gone, don't be an idiot Niko," she warned.

Peeling the towel off his face, Nikolai smiled, "Okay, I behave. Perhaps I should find knife from kitchen and welding mask? Perhaps that scare you all the way to death?"

"Not funny," Mei pouted. She put on her best indignant face and marched back to her chair, ignoring the gentle baiting from the burly Russian. "Now, if you don't mind, *some* of us have important work to get back to, you know, cataloguing new lifeforms, why don't you go back to fixing the kettle?" Mei huffed and started to scribble onto a pad, only she knew that the words she scrawled were nonsensical, and just a show.

Nikolai slapped the side of the doorway and thudded off down the corridor, the sound of him laughing echoed back to Mei.

"Stupid man," she cursed to herself, "he should show more respect to me, I'm the one who everyone will remember when we get back home. They'll build statues of me in town squares, and call their children after me. No one will remember the others, they're just footnotes to my story."

Content, and feeling a little more superior, she closed her pad and eyed up the beaker; a new acceptance speech being mulled over in her head. She coughed and made doe-eyes, "Oh wow! This is…too much…really…" she began to well up, "…this is just so unexpected, coming from such a humble background to being thrust into the spotlight. I'm overwhelmed by this all."

She slapped the table with her hand, "Dammit Mei. No. Too much. Don't overdo it, need a touch of surprise, with sincerity and a smidgen of emotion."

There was a screeching sound from the corridors, of steel nails being dragged down rusting metal, it made her skin crawl. Her mood soured instantly, she huffed and pushed herself away from the desk. "Nikolai, I've told you already, leave me a-"

"Hello Mei," a voice croaked.

# CHAPTER THIRTEEN

The oxygen warning lights had been flashing incessantly for the past ten minutes. Charles and Sabina shared a collective sigh of relief as base camp loomed into view. "Get through the airlock as quickly as possible, I'll be right behind you," Charles gasped through the microphone. Sabina nodded and lurched towards the sealed doors on the side of the collection of modules, cobbled together into an interlinked rectangle.

Charles cut the booster and drifted into the hangar, though it was exposed to the elements, he wanted to check on the Benz first. He punched in the code to the main doors, sealing them shut. Then, with an inanimate carbon rod, smashed the panel until it fizzled and cut out.

The Benz was parked a few metres away, Charles uncoupled the MMU from his main suit and let it drift to the ground, its work complete. Sidling up to the vehicle, he checked the storage bay on the back and saw that it was empty. Reluctantly, he poked his head past the rear passenger section and looked at the drivers' seat.

It was moulded to form a little compartment, waist high if you stood in it. He gagged as he saw clumps of red meat and skull in the foot well, crushed together into a large meatball.

Charles entered the airlock, and waited for it to cycle through its sealing and re-pressurisation cycle. The only thing which made him relax was the sight of Sabina through the viewing panel. She pressed the intercom button on a side panel, "She's here."

He nodded, "The Benz is parked up, we need to be careful, who knows what the hell she is going to do next."

"I'm more concerned about that *thing* she has with her, we don't know what it's fully capable of," Sabina warned, her face scrunched up.

Finally, the airlock light pinged to green, and the seal relaxed, Charles removed his helmet and breathed in the stale air, "That feels better than it should."

"Come on, this place is hardly a labyrinth, we should be able to find her quickly-"

Speakers popped and crackled into life, "Sabina. Charles. You made it. Though if you do not give in, and help with the prime directive, I will have to deal with you too," Dana's voice came out tinny.

Charles fought with his suit, finally managing to disentangle himself from the rigid body. Sabina passed him a lump hammer, "Best be prepared."

"She's got to be in command, let's check there first," Charles hissed. Sabina nodded and the pair slinked down the corridor cautiously. Their journey took them past the biology lab. The door was open, though they could hear the motor firing, then cutting out.

Charles raised a hand to stop, and looked at the bottom of the door. A foot had been hacked off below the ankle and jammed underneath. Toes splayed out either side of the impact site, bent back to unnatural angles.

"My god," he mumbled, hands over his mouth, his brain trying to process everything that he was seeing. The door clunked back into place revealing an abattoir within. Blood was sprayed up the walls, chunks of meat and bone, were stuck in thick congealed patches; in some places, matted hair bristled outwards from tributaries of fluid, like reeds on a riverbank.

Overhead lights strobed, showing Mei sitting in her chair, against the far wall. Her arms were resting on the armrests, palms up. The skin had been sliced open from the middle of her fingerless hands down the middle of her forearms, disappearing under her rolled up sleeves. Shiny crimson roads on the pale blue suit showed the wounds continued unabated.

The skin had been pulled open and was curling over from the edges. Veins and artery had been wrenched free, hanging like silly string from the exposed meat of her arms. Her legs were in a similar state. Except where the incision had been made - up the front of her leg - the shin bone had been scored and partially pulled out.

Her suit had been zipped up, but a crimson Rorschach pattern on the chest, hinted at more horror beneath. Charles swallowed back another wave of vomit and stepped into the room. Though he had already seen too much, the call of the mutilated woman was too much.

Charles looked away, but his eyes were drawn to a test tube rack resting on the edge of the table. Arranged neatly in a row were eight test tubes, each were stuffed with a shorn off finger, the nub of bone glinted as the light flickered. He kicked on the foot doorstop, and after a sickening crack of bones; ending when two toes came loose altogether and flopped free, the door motor fired again and closed off the biologists tomb.

He skated across puddles of blood and void fluid, nearly ending up on the floor as he slipped on a piece of unidentifiable organ. All the while, Mei's head, deformed by terror, sat there, watching.

Flecks of blood airbrushed her smooth skin. Blank eye sockets formed shallow caves of flesh, caring not for the blank nothingness beyond, as her parting had been filled with such terror.

Blood mascara trickled down her cheeks. Her nostrils had been plugged with the squashed orbs, the optical nerves hung out like soaked tampon string. Mei's mouth was open, forceps had been lanced through the skin and held the lips tight against her cheeks.

Her throat had been slashed open, and again, the edges of the wound had been pried into and pulled back, dark red meat with nubs of bone were left on show.

Sat on her lap like a sleeping cat was her other foot, the charm bracelet which jingle-jangled with every step, still looped around the circumference. Blood stained charms stuck to the skin with a tacky red paste.

Blanking out the severed appendage, Charles' trembling fingers reached for the zip, only to find that it was already undone, the flaps of cloth merely resting over one another. Delicately holding the corners of each flap, he began to cautiously open them; the way she was positioned meant Mei's empty sockets looked into his eyes, like a murderous blind date.

Material, starched with dried blood finally parted, as they did, an avalanche of gore and pulped meat slopped from the cloth cage and over Charles' groin, legs and feet. This was the final straw and Charles lurched over to the sink and emptied what little sustenance had been sloshing around his guts. As he opened his eyes, he saw that the plughole was clogged with gristle and tendon, plundered from the dead biologist.

A gentle sobbing and barely suppressed screeches sounded from the doorway. Charles skidded across the slick floor and pulled Sabina in closed, turning her from the bloodbath, "Shhh, it's okay."

"How is it okay? She's dead Charles! And not in a quietly in the night way. She's been ripped apart, murdered," Sabina replied.

Seeing that Charles was dry-retching, Sabina asked, "Are you okay?"

He nodded and pointed to the end of the corridor, "She's got to be in central. C'mon, it's not far, let's go."

The door to the central command hub was closed, the viewing window had blood smeared over from within, obstructing what was inside. Realising they had little choice but to go in, Charles nodded at Sabina to get ready, and then pushed the door release button. It hissed and slid sideways, revealing a room cloaked in near darkness.

From around the chamber came sparks of light as if a multitude of small firework displays were competing with each other. Charles crept into the room, and searched the wall for the light switch. Stopping just in time before he completed the now exposed electrical circuit.

"She's sabotaged the radio," Sabina murmured, pointing her wrench to the wall where it used to live, which was now spouting sparks and tiny forks of lightning.

"Wait a minute, what's that?" Charles pointed off to the far wall. Previously the home of the generator, which powered the array of equipment in the room, the front panel had been pulled free and something jammed into its bowels.

He sidled into the room, the instant he was inside, the door behind him snapped shut, sealing Sabina outside. She banged on the thick door, Charles jumped up and tried the release button, to no avail.

Using his sleeve, he ran it across the viewing window, trying to remove the gunk. Although it was still smudged and smeared over it, the pair could at least see each other. "Go around," Charles mouthed, pointing to the far doorway. Sabina looked confused at first, but then she unfrowned, nodded and headed off down the corridor.

Charles looked back to the room, it would take a few moments for Sabina to get round, and that was providing she didn't run into Dana. Where the hell was Nikolai? Typical that the first time there was a fight to be joined, he had disappeared into thin air.

He breathed out and composed himself. There was nothing he could do about that. He wanted to know what had been shoved into the generator, he had some time to kill, so began to creep across the floor.

Each footstep ended in a cracking of glass or pieces of metal squeaking against the floor, grating against his brain. After knocking into the central table, he felt his way around it and continued his slow, but steady approach.

The object had something thrown over it, as Charles tugged at it, he saw that it was a flight suit, he felt for the embossed name badge and waited for something to spark enough to illuminate it, finally, he saw, 'TONEV', it was Nikolai's.

Much like Mei's he had searched through earlier, this too was stiff with dried on blood. Charles let it drop to the floor. Turning back to the generator, he took a sharp intake of breath when he saw that it was the drone that had been unceremoniously rammed into the electrical guts.

"Why don't you just give in and submit Charles? It'd be better that way," Dana asked. From behind him, a dull thud rang out. Slowly, he turned around and looked into the room. A shape formed in front of him, the overhead light popped and flickered into life, revealing Dana standing on the centre table.

Her skin was more pallid and cracked, as if she was a giant scab. Where lumps had been knocked off, blackened flesh lay exposed, her appearance was like an old mouldy wall, held together purely through spores. Her fight suit was now more red than pale blue, through a layer of gore, he could just make out the improvised 'STINKERMAN' name badge.

"What has happened to you?"

Dana stood immobile, her arms hung by her side like an ape, head tilted to one side, an apex predator eyeing up a tasty morsel, "I've been shown how things are Charles, if only you could see what I have, then you would realise the futility of it all."

"Tell me then! Help me understand, this doesn't have to end like this, we can work something out,"

Charles pleaded, he held the hammer tighter.

"You are not capable of understanding Charles. You're nothing more than an insect. I need to complete the prime directive, and you are in the way. I will kill you now Charles, and when you are dead, I will kill Sabina too. Perhaps I will feast on your entrails as the entity charges. Soon, it will have all it needs."

"Don't do this Dana."

She screeched and hunched down, her toes - distended lengths of bone - wrapped around the lip of the table, before she launched and propelled herself towards Charles.

With the move already telegraphed, he took a step to one side and brought the hammer down as she shot past. It connected with her upper spine and he felt something inside of her give way, as the blow landed.

Dana howled and smacked against the broken vending machine. A waterfall of boiling coffee spurted over the back of her head, scalding the skin and making her roar even louder. She tried to stand up, though her hands still worked, anything below her waist was wilted.

She convulsed on the floor, her legs swung like cooked spaghetti, utterly useless. This made her growl, and she flipped over, still sitting on the ground, but looking at Charles.

"Just give up Dana, or whatever the hell you are, what are you going to do? Bite my kneecaps off?"

Charles asked.

Dana propped herself up with one arm, her other, she raised skywards, "You have no idea what you're dealing with Charles." She brought the arm down onto her chest, just below her ribs, causing a crunching sound.

Pushing herself against the vending machine; which had finally stopped covering her in hot beverages, she dug claws into her chest, and began to gouge away. In a frenzy of tearing and ripping, she pulled out chunks of her own blackened flesh and bone, before hurling it at Charles.

He raised an arm to stop being pelted with offal, but was transfixed by the spectacle in front of him. Having removed the meat, she straightened her hand out so it was in a Kung Fu chop pose.

Grinning like a shit eating psychopath, she brought her hand down against the inside of her spine, which had been revealed after her cavity excavation. Another blow smashed one of the vertebrae, and Dana reached inside and twisted herself apart, coming loose mid-back.

Her leg hemisphere slid to the floor, whilst her torso was held aloft as her hands pushed her up. "Oh bugger," Charles muttered, and hoping to get there in time, lunged at her, hammer raised.

Dana swatted it aside with one hand, sending him crashing to the floor. As the hammer clattered and rolled away, Charles skidded on his cheekbone, which made a loud squeaking sound in his head.

He turned onto his back, just in time to see the bipedal Dana lumber towards him like an organic AT-ST. Her hands pinned his ankles to the ground, and she looked down at Charles, who was still a little stunned from his meeting with the floor. Her fat tongue slapped against her charred teeth, "I'm going to make you hurt now Charles."

One hand at a time, she worked her way up his legs. Dana's fingers bit into his skin, causing him to grimace. She reached his groin, cupping him in one hand. Dana began to squeeze, gently at first, before increasing the pressure.

Charles began to scream, "Get off me," he yelled. Ignoring the searing agony in his bollocks, he balled his fist and punched Dana in the face. "Owwww," he yelled, as it connected with a ball of bone. Her head rocked backwards, and she wobbled, pulling again at his testicles.

Dana's other hand pushed down on his chest, and she leered down at him, her rictus grin being slathered by her swollen disgusting tongue. "I don't think you'll be needing these Charles," she rasped and began to twist her groin clamped hand.

Charles began to howl like a stunned pig, his vision began to go red, the pain in his balls was unbearable. It felt as though they were being forced through a cheese grater. He lashed out and shoved his hand in Dana's face, trying to push her away. Her tongue ran up one of his fingers, like someone had a cold dank flannel, and was trying to clean him.

Knowing it was very much now or never, he grabbed hold of her tongue in one hand, and held her throat in the other. As the tongue hand pulled, the throat hand pushed.

Dana began to gag, the hold on his nutsack finally relented, never had such a joyous feeling been felt. She tried to fight back, her hands latched around his, the talons scratching the flesh, trying to get him off.

Charles had one thing on his side, momentum. With her hands now in self-defence mode, he was able to push her off of him and onto what remained of her back. He smacked her against the ground, causing her arms to relinquish their hold. He leant forwards and pinned her shoulders with his knees, before recommencing the pull and push motion.

Charles took a deep breath and pulled harder, something inside Dana cracked and split, her tongue began to unfurl. With one last wrench, he ripped her tongue clean out of her head and threw it behind him. Her face now replete with a huge bloody crater, Dana's jaws had been torn open, and her lower jaw hung useless against her throat.

Still holding her to the floor, he used his free arm to elbow Dana in the face, over and over again. He lost himself to the motion, finally coming to when he felt his elbow hitting the metal floor. Looking down at the desolation of her face, he finally let go. Her skull was now a bowl of bone, filled with red slop. Charles fell onto his haunches, breathing hard.

He struggled to catch his breath, wiping his brow

with his sleeve. Charles then stuck a hand into his pants and felt his tender meat and two veg, making sure there was the correct amount remaining, "Thank god for-"

Dana's head snapped up, an approximation of a laugh bubbled out of her smashed in face. She pulled off the end of her index finger, discarding the chalk like finger-tip, before jabbing it into Charles neck. She gurgled a, "Tag, you're it Charles," before collapsing like a lost game of Jenga.

Charles fell backwards, clutching the wound. It felt warm, sweat beaded off his head, the room undulated around him, before his eyes blinked and fell shut. "Oh bugger," he whimpered, before passing out.

# CHAPTER FOURTEEN

Clouds stretched as far as Charles could see, a pale blue sky with a red tinge was painted overhead. No sound except for wind, which blew right through him. Like a majestic eagle he soared, borne aloft on a current, skating the underbelly of heaven itself.

Was he dead? Is this the transition from one world to the next? Who would be waiting for him? Questions ran around his mind, from the mundane to the most profound. He struggled to tug upon their very thread, which only extinguished the fragility of the supposition.

"Hello Charles."

Frantically, he looked around, yet could see no form of his own, he was the wind, the very air, a phantom travailing the skies, scoffing at the trivialities of existence.

There was nothing and no one up here with him, just endless sky. Beyond a thin veil of black and grey, shone the roiling sun. Molten plasma ejected from the

surface, lashing the angry swelling seas of fire.
"Do you like the view Charles?
I've been informed by organics, that it is
aesthetically pleasing.
Though, of course, no one has seen this for
some time."

Charles gave in, "What do you mean?"
"Let me show you Charles."

Banking sharply downwards, Charles transitioned into a cloud. Beads of perspiration and mist coated his vision. Then, he was through, looking up at cloud paunches, his exit signalled by wisps of trailing vapour. Charles thought back to when he was a child, tracing white trails across the sky, believing them to be space shuttles. His father shattered the illusion with the mundane truth, but it was always his first thought. Not people being carried across the world, but explorers breaking free from the yoke of the Earth, reaching for the unknown.

The view below was of sprawling plains of ochre, lined by tar lanes awash with teeming life, all vying to be first, carrying their burden forever onwards. The country sprawl yielded its bounty to a city, grey blocks encroached along its borders, linking the thin black trails with wider avenues and canals.

There was just so much motion, even from his viewpoint. Everything swarmed, striving to get somewhere, never ceasing. Signs of industry spewed from metal monoliths. Great swathes of acrid gritty smoke were puffed into the air like a festering wound in zero gravity.

Still they descended.

A craft of a delta wing construction soared above them, jinking this way and that. Golden rays lanced through rent open patches of clouds, and glinted off the shiny silver body. Etched on its chassis were painted figures which he could not discern.

Like realising he were in someone else's dream, Charles became panicked. He could make out red roots to the fields beneath him. Buildings blotted the horizon which registered no familiarity. A river ran below, yet instead of blue, it ran like mercury. Thick waves rose and lapped against the bank, depositing a crystalline goo, which pooled together and slid back into the febrile tide.

"Where am I?" Charles asked flatly, seeing nothing of his home in this place.

"This is Solus Four Charles,
I believe your species refer to it as Mars."

"When was this? This isn't Mars now, you must be mistaken," Charles replied, looking around at a flock of multi-winged animals struggling to flee from the city below. Harsh grunts echoed from their braying breasts. Their chunky forms seemed at odds with the graceful way they took to the skies.

"This is the end Charles.
Look."

Scouring the sky, Charles saw a long cylindrical object lance through a nearby cloud, its tail aflame. Adorned on its flanks was a symbol. Scorched red and white stripes were the backdrop to a white star sitting on a blue square.

As it threaded the ethereal cloud, the fiery tail blazed anew, increasing the velocity.

"But it's headed straight for the city."

The rocket, with its fresh burst of power flew towards the heart of the grey blister, puckered in the ground. The vitality and bustle which seemed so effervescent, ceased.

Where there was a flow, now there was only reluctant acceptance.

A settling of a lingering debt.

Though some errant scraps seeked escape, the majority simply stopped.

Gazing skywards.

To their end.

A brilliant explosion of white ignited the air. Where the weapon once hung, suspended in the air, it was now replaced by an orb of pure light. It burst and blossomed outwards. A pall of thunder, like Thor cracking Mjolnir on an anvil. It was deafening. The shockwaves themselves could be seen as they sped across the sky, bending the air and causing the flock of avian to careen to the ground.

As the booming rippled outwards, the orb contracted in on itself. When it could no longer contain the energy within, it exploded once more. This time, it cast forth waves of fire. This rolled over the plains first, singing them to a blackened crisp.

The thin capillaries of commerce which ringed the

countryside disappeared under a dousing of molten slag, wiping clean the industry of those who tilled the lands and had laid the roads for their forebears.

The apocalyptic wave then washed over the outlying buildings of the city. Towers blew out from the bottom up, rings of fire exploding from each level in turn, jettisoning out charred specks of ebony. It was unstoppable. Like a blanket, existence was doused in flame, entire districts, identifiable as individual states, were wiped out in one stroke.

As the last vestiges of destruction poured over the horizon, the only sound was that of the wind. This time though it howled in vengeance. Mourning the loss of equilibrium.

Charles felt something inside crack, and blow out, what was a controlled voyage, now descended into a spiralling smoking whirlwind. With a thud, he smacked into the ground.

All around him, everything burned. Buildings were eviscerated husks, guts bared to the carrion. Clay figures, some hunched together, others pointing towards the sky stood as petrified ornaments. Details and differences bleached from their covering, all turned into amorphous statues. Frozen in the moment of their extinction.

The sky above spat acid rain, causing the brimstone to bubble and crack. Steam and smoke merged together above him, thickening.

"What the bloody hell happened?"

"An execution Charles.

This planet was designated as a death world.
It is my duty to facilitate an extinction level event to these worlds.
If I cannot utilise their own technology to do so, then I use alternate means."

"Who does? What gives you the right to do this? All those people, gone, for what? This doesn't make any sense," Charles shouted.

"There are planets which are teeming with a virus Charles.
Oxygen is a known poison across the galaxy, the effects of its ingestion are catastrophic to the organics that breathe it in.
It causes paranoia, and a sense of false entitlement.
Upon primitive belief structures, the organics which inhabit these worlds consume without thought to the consequence.
They kill not just the other indigenous organic lifeforms, but also their own.
They are contaminated.
We tried to integrate them into the universe, but that only ended in war.
So now, we cleanse them.
Your species is mirrored across the known universe.
It is a familiar template, an easy one to be replicated.
Ordinarily, your physiology would enable you to be near immortal.
Unshackled by the pursuits of the oxygen addiction, a higher purpose is easily attainable.

It is why the organic you referred to as Dana, did not perish upon contact with the atmosphere on Solus Four."

Through the gloom, a beam of light tore across the sky, fighting to get out of the atmosphere and the dying world.

"What's that?" Charles asked.

"An error Charles.
In my hubris, I failed to detect a craft capable of interplanetary travel.
For two hundred thousand of your Solus Three years, I have lay here in the rubble.
Ruing my mistake.
Though I toyed with some of those who survived my wrath, my unfulfilled mission parameters vexed me.
That a handful of those marked for death, had escaped.
But now, I can complete my mission.
With some assistance."

The flash of light disappeared into a cloud, now a baleful monitor, a moment of realisation ran across Charles' mind, "They're heading for Earth."

Another explosion rumbled through him, the crust belched and complained. A crevasse opened up beneath him, Charles felt air below, teetering on the edge. A whip crack across the land shook the ground, and he was pulled to its fracked bosom.

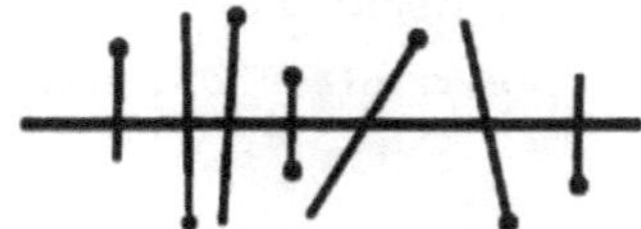

"Charles, CHARLES!" Sabina, through with putting on her best bedside manner, slapped the unconscious man across the cheek.

Like being stirred from fitful sleep by an alarm, Charles fluttered his eyelids open. Two shapes, stolen away by shadows, loomed over him, "What?" he asked, still groggy.

Sabina held her hand out and pulled him up to the sitting position, "Are you alright?" Nikolai asked, his burly frame returning into focus.

Slowly, Charles nodded, he clamped a hand to his neck and felt a bandage, "I saw…"

"What did you see?" Sabina demanded.

"I saw the end," Charles moaned. He looked up, into Sabina's blue eyes, "I know what that thing is trying to do."

# CHAPTER FIFTEEN

Nikolai play punched Charles on the shoulder, "I must get back to command, need to assess damage to systems. Don't go getting hurt again huh?" With that, he shuffled uncomfortably, and headed out of medical.

Charles craned his neck, making sure he had gone. Conspiratorially, he beckoned Sabina to him, "I saw something Sabina. Whilst I was out…this thing, this drone, it wiped this planet out."

Sabina folded her arms, "Really? And how did it do that exactly?"

"It must be able to manipulate electronic equipment, said that if it can't do that, it finds a way. It always finds a way. Next stop was Earth," Charles winced and dabbed at the bandage to see if he was still leaking blood.

"Hmm, makes sense I guess, must've connected to Dana through her intercom, how did it speak to you though?" she asked.

Charles laid back on the propped up bed, "Through Dana, some connection she had, before she died, I don't know. There's something else though."

Sabina pried Charles fingers away, and checked the wound herself, satisfied that it was closing up, "Go on, I'm listening."

"It said it needs help to do this now…it said that Nikolai was under its control," Charles panted, looking into her eyes.

She looked back, unblinking, searching for something hidden beyond what was there, after a moment of uncomfortable silence, she sighed, "Sounds like it could be true, he came into medical the night Dana was brought in, said he'd cut his finger when he was checking the drone out."

"Isn't that wh-"

Sabina nodded, "Dana said that she let it take some blood from her, yes, I know. I've got an idea. Perhaps it transmits some kind of nanobot into organic lifeforms? Maybe it manipulates people that way? I took some blood from Dana and Nikolai when they came in that day."

"That's excellent, if you check them, you can see if there is anything that links the pair together, that's good thinking," Charles swung his legs off the bed. Sabina pulled a syringe from a stainless steel tray, removing the plastic cap she held in front of Charles, "What do you think you're going to do with that?"

"You said it yourself, they came into contact with

the drone."

"Yes, and?"

"You came into contact with Dana, you're the only one who has seen these visions, that I know of anyway."

Charles went to stand up, "I'm not liking your tone Sabina," he grunted. She pushed him back to the sitting position.

"I'm going to need some of your blood too, only right that I check you out as well. You know, for the sake of completeness."

He glowered at her as if she had broken the Sunday best teapot, through clenched jaw, he grumbled, "Fine, if you must."

She jabbed him before he could change his mind and pulled the plunger back, withdrawing a vial of blood, "First test passed, it doesn't look like hers did." Sabina peeled off a plaster and stuck it over the puncture mark, "No lollipop I'm afraid. I'll go and have a look at this n-"

The speaker burst into life, "Charles, Sabina…you better come to command. I have good news and bad news."

Sabina scribbled Charles name onto a label on the side of the tube and placed it into a rack, next to the other samples, "Guess this will have to wait until later."

She helped Charles up and the pair stumbled to the doorway, he put an unsteady hand against the metal frame, "You go on, I'll catch you up, I think I need to vomit." Covering his mouth with his hand, he staggered down the corridor towards the bathroom.

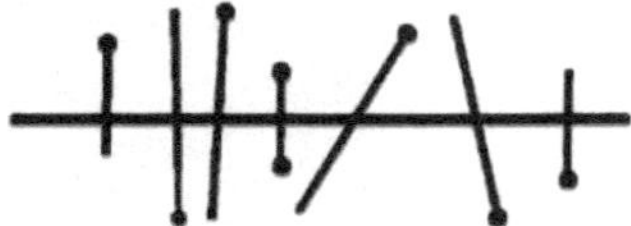

As Sabina entered the murky command module, the fluorescent lights flickered into life, revealing Nikolai rooting around in the guts of an underfloor panel, torch clamped between his teeth. A muted cheer echoed through the floor as he stood up, unaware that he had company, "Sorry," he mumbled, "no lights was annoying me. Where is Charles?"

"He'll be along in a minute, he's just throwing up," Sabina said with faux cheerfulness. She pointed at the drone, still jammed into the generator, "What's that still doing there?"

Nikolai shrugged, "It is buried in tight, Dana was stronger than she looked, I tried to remove, but it wouldn't budge. Anyway, that is not problem."

"Then what is, Nikolai?" Charles asked. He trotted into the room, a wad of folded paper towels in hand, mopping the corners of his mouth.

The torch was placed on the central console, "Bad news first. The air scrubbers have been damaged, it will take approximately one day, maybe two, to fix them. We have enough oxygen for twelve hours."

Sabina ran fingers through her cropped brown

hair, "That's just great."

"Surely that's not too bad, Dana showed that we don't oxygen," Charles piped up.

The other two looked at him, "I do not want to look like I am skeleton Charles. Besides, we may survive, but our supplies would not. They would be contaminated, we starve to death or get ill. No. No good."

"Okay, so what's the good news?" Sabina asked.

"No good news. Only more bad news. I think we need to go. Whatever this thing is," Nikolai pointed to the metal tube humming from within a mass of snaking, fizzing electrical cables, "it is not good. I say we leave it here, get back home. No good can come of staying here. Ask Dana, or Sanjay, or Mei. No. We go. Now."

Charles looked at Sabina knowingly, "How long would it take to prep the Venturer?"

She rolled her eyes up, working out timings, "I think we could get ready to go in maybe two hours, once the primary checks are done."

"Good, then we leave. I go prepare ship," Nikolai said firmly, setting off towards the exit.

Charles stood in his way, "Hold on there Nikolai, old chap. I think Sabina should prep for launch, me and you can pack up the essentials here. Don't you agree Sabina?"

"Yes, I think that works better, I've got a quick check to do before I can suit up, you two start getting everything we need for transportation back home.

Don't forget Mei's findings, if they're still there. Least we can do is submit those for her."

Nikolai looked from Sabina to Charles, "Fine. Now, please, can we go? This place gives me creeps." He cast a sideways glance at the drone, then thudded off down the corridor, towards the biology lab.

"Does that give you enough time to do the test?" Charles asked.

Sabina nodded, "Yes, it will take half an hour to complete the process, but I can get the results remotely to my gauntlet, I don't need to be on site."

"Good work, I'll go and start packing up, the sooner we go, the better. He's right about one thing, this place gives me the creeps."

# CHAPTER SIXTEEN

"Okay guys, I'm in the Venturer, starting the pre-launch checks now. Please. Don't take too long. Bring only what we need, leave everything else, they're gonna have to clean this place with fire when they come back," Sabina chirped into the intercom.

Charles pressed the earpiece into his ear and nodded along, "Okay Nikolai, let's get this done." He wandered into the biology lab. Mei's mutilated body had been taken from the chair and laid on the floor. A stained blanket covered her from head to hacked off ankles. Two lumps on her midriff signalled where her feet were.

With an open sports bag, he'd pilfered from under Sanjay's bed, Charles rifled through the contents of a tall cabinet. Reams of statistical data, nothing but meaningless numbers and line charts hung in suspended pockets. Not having the slightest clue as to what any of it hinted at, Charles skipped past it.

A few full notebooks were plundered from the top

drawer, and a half empty bottle of Bacardi was liberated from under a pile of blank forms. Charles headed to the table and saw, that although the body had been removed, Mei's fingers were still stuffed into the test tubes. He covered the rack with a sodden towel and rooted through the desk drawers.

Aside from a handful of flash drives, his search was fruitless, nothing but more printouts of endless readings. Charles slammed the drawer shut and spun around on the chair. He saw a laptop lying on the floor, in a congealed puddle of blood. Peeling it free, he wiped it on the edge of the blanket and stashed it in the bag.

Opening the fridge, he saw row upon row of test tubes, complete with various coloured liquid in. Charles picked up the closest one, and read the label, Mei's unintelligible handwriting made the job impossible.

"Don't worry about them," Nikolai yelled from the doorway, "we have nowhere to put them on the ship. Just make sure you have data from laptop, and we should be okay."

Charles nodded and replaced the tube back into the fridge, he closed the door and stood up, "You got everything Nikolai?"

Nikolai nodded and waved his arm, "Come on, let's leave this place. Smells bad. We go home now." The Russian slapped the metal doorframe and disappeared from view.

As Charles made one last check, his intercom

earpiece beeped, "Hello?"

"Charles, this is Sabina. I've got the results back…you were right. Though it's not identical, and I'm putting that down to her exposure to the atmosphere, there is some kind of alien parasite in Nikolai's blood, the same as Dana."

Charles watched as Nikolai punched in the door code for the pre-airlock chamber. The door hissed and yawned open, he stood there waiting, beckoning Charles to hurry up. "Charles? Do you copy?"

"Yes, I do, thanks. I'm here with Nikolai now," he muttered, Nikolai furrowing his brow at the Englishman holding his finger in his ear.

"What do we do?" she asked.

"Uh-huh, we should be on our way shortly."

Nikolai mouthed, "Is that Sabina?"

Charles nodded and pulled a face, "We'll figure something out, we're about to suit up. See you soon."

Nikolai grew impatient, "Come on! Hurry up, or I'll leave you here with that thing."

Charles punched a code into the number pad on his gauntlet, he pulled it close to his face and whispered into it. "Is that Sabina again? You know that you two should be on the all-crew channel, don't you?" Nikolai shouted at him.

Grinning like a deranged lunatic, Charles dropped the bag of gear onto the floor, "It is your turn to die now Nikolai."

Nikolai frowned, "What do you mean? This is no time for funny business. Come on."

Charles marched up to the Russian, his nose coming to rest at the same height as Nikolai's chin, "Such a primitive race Nikolai, your kind has learnt nothing since you fled this place. You should have all died then."

"No…you're like Dana, aren't you?" Nikolai asked, gently teasing the bag from his shoulder.

"Primitive and stupid Nikolai. So very fragile too. We were able to pull the others apart so easily, you should've heard them begging us to stop. To leave them alone. We couldn't. We wouldn't. You are nothing more than a virus. You must be destroyed," Charles grinned.

Nikolai cracked his knuckles, "You know I have to stop you, don't you?"

"You know nothing about what will come to pass Nikolai. Your family will burn in nuclear fire, their skin peeled from them."

"What are you talking about? How? Tell me the truth, tell me everything."

"I don't know what you mean Nikolai. We *are* truth. We are the judge. Sentence is passed already. We will complete the prime directive."

"That *thing* is in you? Is it in your blood? I will have to kill you Charles. I'll butcher you like you made Dana kill Mei," Nikolai growled.

"You killed Mei when you left her alone. You're like your species, a coward," Charles continued his goading.

"You know nothing about me. But I know now

that I must kill you," Nikolai bellowed. He swung his fist, connecting with Charles cheek, who let out a scream. The punch sent Charles spinning through the air, landing in a heap on the floor.

Like a shark on a piece of chump, Nikolai was on the prone figure like a flash, lashing out with fist and boot. Charles fell limp, not attempting to stymy the assault, he seemed accepting of what was being meted out.

Nikolai picked up Charles head, already matted with blood and slammed it against the floor, he went to strike him again, but pulled out of the punch. "No, I leave you here with that *thing*. If you're here, you can't do anything little man."

Releasing him, Charles slapped against the floor, he began to cackle.

# CHAPTER SEVENTEEN

Sabina clicked the intercom off and checked the results again. Clear as day, there it was, Charles was fine, whilst Nikolai's sample had the same tell-tale signs of infection as she had found within Dana. How would they deal with him?

At least, between the two of them, they should be able to restrain Nikolai in some way, incapacitate him. If it came to it, they'd kill him. It wouldn't be her first choice, but after the grisly sights she had witnessed, she knew that it might be the only way.

The earpiece warbled, throwing out a chorus line of static, Sabina tapped it, as if it would rectify the fault. Through the flurry of white noise, Nikolai's voice emerged, ""You know…………don't you?"

Sabina spoke into the mic, "Hello? Nikolai?" In between squalls of static, the conversation stuttered along, the pair unaware or unable to hear her.

She heard Charles reply, "…know…about what……………"

"…talking about……truth……everything…"

"I don't know what you mean Nikolai………………"

Sabina twisted dials, fiddled with the volume controls, desperately trying to clear the distortion from the audio. As she tried to fine tune the channel, Nikolai's voice broke through, "…I will have to kill you Charles. I'll butcher you like…………Mei…"

She gasped, she couldn't believe it. When they had found Mei's body, she had naturally assumed it was Dana. Personal grievance or no, the way she had been ripped apart, suggested that the twisted thing that Dana had become, was responsible.

Nikolai?

Then it hit her. Where was he when Mei was killed? He was alone with her at the station the entire time. He had more than enough time to do the atrocities meted out to her.

Charles replied, his voice sounded sombre, yet sincere, "You killed Mei………you're………a coward."

Another burst of static nearly made Sabina rip the earpiece out, then Nikolai, his unmistakeable voice thick with anger, roared, "…now…I must kill you." There was a scream, and then the audio went dead.

She sat there stunned, conflicting emotions trading blows in her head like a couple of prizefighters. She should go down there, help Charles out, two against one, though that one was built like a brick shithouse and more than likely has already gotten the better of the Brit.

Then play it cool, her brain suggested, lull Nikolai into a false sense of security, he's got to sleep, surely? When he does, stick him with a cocktail of drugs and flush him out of the airlock.

But what if that thing controlling him doesn't need sleep? What if she went to administer the drugs and she was the one who was pitched out into the infinity of space? She could be the only thing that stands between Earth and total annihilation.

Dammit.

Charles had tried to warn her too, but instead of believing him, she did what she always did, got cynical and followed her head. Now look where she was, sat in the pilot seat of a ship on Mars, with a killer on the loose who is under some kind of alien control. It was giving her a headache.

Then her earpiece popped, "Sabina, this is Nikolai. Am suited up, ready to enter, please open airlock."

Sabina breathed out, "Of course Nikolai, give me a moment."

*Shit, shit, shit, I could just leave him there? But didn't Dana say that it overrode her suit control. Right now, he doesn't know that I know about him. If he realises, that thing will just open the door anyway.*

"Sabina? Hurry up, it is not safe," Nikolai demanded.

An idea hit her, "Nikolai, we've got a problem with the auxiliary booster. Readout says the fuel line is non-responsive, could you check it out please?"

There was a loud sigh down the microphone, "Fine, but we must hurry. Must leave this place. I'll go now."

Sabina turned to the ignition control panel, and opened the switch gates, Nikolai spoke again, "I am here by booster, fuel line intact."

"Okay, thanks, could you just check the igniter, still getting an alarm on the panel, without that, we won't be going anywhere."

"Fine, hang on. I think I can just reach inside with my arm," Nikolai crooned into the speaker.

Her finger hovered over the ignition switch.

*There's no other way.*

She flicked the switch down, Nikolai's screams filled her ears. Below the craft, the Russian had no time to retract his appendage from the narrow exhaust pipe. Heat, enough to burn through lead engulfed his arm, reducing it to ash within seconds. The blowback pushed Nikolai out and into the path of the booster rocket.

Fire licked at his helmet. The last thing he saw was what looked like fire rain, cascading down from a tube. It chewed through his visor and disintegrated his face. Sabina clicked the ignition off. Nikolai's lifeless body thudded against the belly of the craft before gently floating away, borne aloft on a gentle breeze.

Sabina sat in her chair, a tear tracked down her cheek. That was it, she was alone. Carrying out one last run through, she checked to make sure that everything was ready.

"Sabina?" a croaky voice asked.

"Charles? Is that you? Thank god, I thought you were dead."

She heard laughing, "Not quite. Nikolai gave me a bit of a pasting, but I'm okay. A few cracked ribs I think, and my looks have been diminished somewhat. Where is…where is…you know…he?"

Sabina looked down into her hands, "He's dead, I think, vapourised by the rocket. Look, just hurry up and get over here, okay? I'm not losing anyone else today."

"Of course," Charles coughed, "I'll just get Mei's data and I'll be over, give me twenty minutes, okay?"

"Affirmative, see you soon," Sabina's head knocked the back of her seat with relief.

She was sure they were going to make it, they'd be safe.

# CHAPTER EIGHTEEN

The craft burned away from the red planet, punching through the atmosphere. Sabina eased up on the throttle and began to type in the co-ordinates that would take them both home.

She reflected on her time there, for the most part, it had been pretty dull. Her job was to get them there and back again, and to fix people up when they had a medical concern. Aside from a few sprains, one of the nastiest things she had to deal with was when Sanjay had burned his hand when preparing their dinner one night.

A part of her wondered whether he'd done it intentionally. Sanjay had whinged that it was not a man's job. She remembered the first time he'd said that, her blood had boiled and she nearly force fed him a whole plate.

Still, he was a good man, aside from his old fashioned views. He was funny and though a tad on the self-serving side, looked out for everyone, especially when they fell into a low period. That was Dana all over. After the first few months on the surface, she had become a morose snidey shadow of her former self. Always trying to demean Mei's work, or belittle it.

Whilst Mei had gotten on her nerves - which was an inevitability living in such close quarters – she had found the ditzy biologist to be a good friend.

Nikolai though, she shed no tears over. He had made it clear at all times, that she was merely the co-pilot. No, he deserved what was coming to him, she was sure of that. "How's it going Sabina?" Charles asked, bobbing up beside her in zero gravity.

She smiled at him, the bumbling gent who somehow always managed to put his foot in it, yet only meant well, "Nearly done, then we just have to idle away the next few months. Hope you remembered to pick the cards up before you got out of there."

Charles bowed, "But of course, I might even teach you Gin Rummy, once the atmosphere levels out, might be a tad awkward otherwise. I'm just going to stow away Mei's things properly, won't be a tick." With that, he floated down the length of the cockpit, before hauling himself through the doorway and into the belly of the ship which housed the living quarters.

With the final checks done, Sabina activated the autopilot and waited as the craft juddered and shifted on its axis, pointing towards home. She smiled, *nearly got it bang on, not bad for a girl huh Nikolai?*

She unclipped her seatbelt and switched the dashboard to standby, they wouldn't need this now until they were within a few thousand miles of earth, where she would finally get to land it herself.

The door to the cockpit closed with a dull thud, and Sabina rolled through the corridor. As she passed one of the bedrooms, she saw Charles struggle to store Mei's blood spattered laptop, and a bag of flash drives, "I'm going to fire up the artificial atmosphere," she voxed, garnering a thumbs up from Charles in reply.

Her boot magnetised and she clamped onto the deck, the stern cargo area looked so barren. She remembered the vast amount of crates and stores that they had turned up with, now nothing more than a pittance of supplies. Least with just the two of them, food wouldn't be a problem. Sabina pulled the console down and typed in the command, a warning claxon sounded, near deafening her, even through her suit.

Gradually, she could feel everything sinking. It was like a lake being drained, revealing an Atlantisian city beneath. Her arms flopped by her sides, motor movement restored. She watched as the $O^2$ levels rose, and the display indicated that the artificial atmosphere was nearly complete.

Like a cake baking in the oven, a bell rang, signalling that the air was now breathable. She disconnected her helmet, and gladly removed it. Though she never dared utter it to her trainers, it gave her terrible claustrophobia, if it wasn't for the wide aspect afforded, she doubted she would've made it past basic training.

Sabina started to remove the heavy suit, and stomped over to the storage lockers at the far end of the bay. Each crew members name was machine punched onto a strip of steel which was in turn screwed to the front of each locker. She opened hers and began to pack away her gear. Having stepped out of her suit, she hung it up and closed the door. The bolt bounced off the catch. Irritated, Sabina caught the door and slammed it shut. "Damn thing."

As it reverberated, the door to Mei's locker creaked and opened a crack. Sabina tutted, trillions of dollars to get them there, and they skimped on a lousy door lock. She grabbed hold of the door and wrenched it open, ready to slam it closed, harder than her own, out of principle.

With the door wide open, she saw a sports bag pushed into the bottom of the locker. Unless Mei's ghost had decided to pack something away in her stead, it should be empty. Curious, she knelt down and pulled the bag out of the locker. Whatever it was, it was heavy, it clanged against the floor. With her brain trying to work out what the hell it was, she grabbed hold of the zip.

"What are you doing Sabina?" Charles asked, standing at the entrance to the cargo bay, still dressed in his full atmospheric suit, helmet and all.

"Nothing, just packing my stuff away and Mei's

locker opened, she had this bag in there, wondered what is in it, that's all," she answered.

"Don't open the bag Sabina," Charles warned.

She turned to look at him, he was part obscured by the open locker door. He began to march towards her purposefully. Sabina ripped the zip towards her and opened up the flaps, she gasped in shock. Nestled in amongst a blood covered flight suit was the drone. "How did…" the words drifted off, the footsteps grew closer.

She felt a thwack as Charles' gauntlet swung and caught her square on the cheekbone, she fell backwards and clattered against the locker. Charles looked down at her, "I told you Sabina. Don't open the bag. Why did you have to do that for? Your job was complete, I was going to study you on our voyage, see if your species has any redeeming features. You may have been the last human left alive, before I throttled you to death."

Sabina's head spun, a trio of images swam in front of her, she lashed out feebly at the closest one, missing and wafting her hand in thin air. Charles snatched her wrist, "Instead Sabina, I get to kill you now. You disappoint me."

She shook her head clear, "Yeah? Well, you're not all metal are you?" With that, she brought her boot up and connected with Charles' testicles, doubling him over in pain. Eager to seize the advantage, she grabbed the air pipe which ran round the back of his helmet and smashed his head against the metal locker.

There was a loud crack, Sabina pulled him back and administered his face to the locker once more. This time there was a smash, thick chunks of glass tinged off the floor.

Sabina smacked Charles against the locker again, sending a fountain of blood spraying over the brushed steel. "Had enough yet? Disappointed now?"

Charles fell slack in her grasp, she let go and put her boot through the destroyed visor and kicked him in the face.

After a few more lusty blows, she stood back, panting. Charles lay motionless on the floor, a swatch of bloodied skin was plastered over his face where his nose used to be. Hands rapped against the floor, trying to engender movement, but getting no response from the central nervous system. Sabina stood over him, "You disappoint *me* Charles, I'll go get you a little something. Was thinking I'd need it for Nikolai, but it'll do you just fine."

She jogged towards the corridor, as she got to within a few feet, the door whooshed closed. Sabina slammed against it, she tried to dig her fingernails underneath it to heave it up, it didn't budge at all.

"Hello Sabina, looks like you have some fight in you after all."

Sabina turned back to the room to see Charles closing Mei's locker and wrenching the handle up to stop it popping open. He turned to face her, he was covered in blood and splinters of bone, "You cannot win Sabina. We could make a show of it, but the end is inevitable, so I think I'll save both of us the trouble."

"What the hell do you mean?" Sabina screamed.

Warning lights began to ring out along the ceiling, Sabina looked to the side doors, "No, please, don't."

"It will be quick Sabina, in roughly twenty nine seconds you will be dead. Then I can continue on course and complete the prime directive."

Sabina sunk to her knees. Charles, unconscious, yet mouthing the words sat next to her, fingers stiffly stroked her hair. As the sirens wailed and lights strobed, the cargo door cracked open and pulled the pair towards the tiny fissure. The lockers which were bolted to the floor, shook and rattled.

Forced between the cargo bay and the vacuum of space, Charles body was dragged through the hole first. His body was broken and mangled to fit through the opening. Sabina held her breath and slipped through the gap and into the void. As she cartwheeled away from the speeding craft, she saw Charles' face ice up, frozen like one of the cartoons she used to watch as a little girl in Bochum.

Her body floated around and she saw the blazing boosters push the ship away from her.

Blood turned to ice, and her heart stopped. The pair danced in the eternal night.

# CHAPTER NINETEEN

"Another glorious morning Ted, what did you and Nancy get up to last night?" Malcolm asked, reclining on his chair.

Ted laid the headset down, "Not much Malc, she rustled up some spicy chicken wings, we had the Donovan's come round. Nancy and Penny nattered on for an hour about the kids, whilst me and Herb sat on the porch drinking a few cold ones."

"That sounds like a mighty fine evening, got to make the most of these long days now huh?"

Ted nodded, "That you do, how ab-"

A sound like crashing waves sang through the headset, the two men exchanged a puzzled look, "About damn time, we ain't heard a peep since they left. If it weren't for the telemetry readings, I'd have feared the worst by now," Malcolm said, he nodded across to Ted, "Let's go welcome them folks back, sure are a lot of people waiting to hear their voices."

Ted spun around and shoved the headset on,

pulling the mic in close, he stifled a sneeze, then said. "Pathfinder, this is Houston control, we have you on audio and tracking. Do you copy, over?"

Static fizzed through the speakers. Malcolm shoved another piece of nicotine gum into his mouth, "Guess I chose the wrong week to quit smoking."

Twirling dials, Ted spoke into the mic again, "I say again. Pathfinder, this is Houston control. Do you copy? Over."

The speaker mewled and popped;
"This is Pathfinder Houston."


# The End.

# ABOUT THE AUTHOR

Exploring the world, dressed only in his threadbare socks, and cheery disposition, Duncan P. Bradshaw, seeks a better tomorrow, today. With his trusty wife, Debbie, and their two cats, Rafa and Pepe, they form a mean team.

Whilst Duncan distracts door-to-door salesman with his witty banter, the felines are ready, above them, itching to rend them limb from limb. Once dealt with, they are ground down to a lumpy paste, which is used as mortar on new-build housing in neighbouring counties.

Check out his website:

http://duncanpbradshaw.co.uk/

Go and give him a like on that there Facebook:

https://www.facebook.com/duncanpbradshaw

# MORE TITLES FROM

It's the thirteenth annual Lou Gehrig awards. Four B-list celebrity virologists vie to claim the Locked In Syndrome cup and get mulched down to form their disease for mass distribution.

A disease hipster takes centre stage on a night when a blast from the past threatens to turn his ordered, pus filled life upside down. In order to blow open a deep rooted conspiracy, he must team up with a disgraced one time child star who wants another shot at the big time, and clear his sullied name.

Together, they're going to show people the real meaning of a meltdown.

"You're completely at the mercy of his strange imagination and all the eccentric oddities that his curious mind can conjure up. Indeed, it quickly becomes apparent that the only way you'll be able to wade through the veritable quagmire of lunacy is by simply succumbing to the madness."
-   DLS Reviews

Hungover, dumped and late for work.

On an ordinary day, one of these would be a bad morning, but today Jim Taylor also has to contend with the zombie apocalypse.

Follow Jim during twenty four hours of Day One, as he and his zombie obsessed brother deal with the undead, a doomsday cult and maniacs in their quest to get to their parents, win his girlfriend back and for them to instigate 'The Plan'.

Worlds will collide and fall apart in a Class Three outbreak.

'This, ladies and gentlemen, is a classic. This is a book that all people who read horror stories need to have on their shelves. Horror. Yes. Comedy. Yes. Does it mix well? Absolutely yes.'
-   Confessions of a Reviewer

# CLASS FOUR

## Those Who Survive

In the months after a deadly virus has swept across the planet, an eight year old boy and his appointed protector live from day to day. After a chance encounter they head for sanctuary. To get there, they will have to run the gauntlet of the inhabitants of this new world.

Ruled over by The Gaffer, a group of survivors holed up in a derelict factory struggle to maintain order and stability. Inside, those affected the most share their stories, hoping to come to terms with what has happened and what they've lost.

However, a clandestine operative in their midst lays the groundwork for an assault, the likes of which none of them have ever seen or could hope to prepare for.

These are the stories of those who survive.

'Class Four is a total blast of a novel from beginning to end and, like its predecessor, is one of the better interpretations of the zombie apocalypse.'
-    Ginger Nuts of Horror

# heXagram

We are all made of stars.

When an ancient Inca ritual is interrupted, it sets in motion a series of events that will echo through five hundred years of human history. Many seek to use the arcane knowledge for their own ends, from a survivor of a shipwreck, through to a suicide cult.

Yet...the most unlikeliest of them all will succeed.

"Hexagram is a visceral journey through the dark nooks and crannies of human history. Lovecraftian terror merges with blood sacrifice, suicide cults and body horror as Bradshaw weaves an intricate plot into an epic tale of apocalyptic dread."
**- Rich Hawkins, author of The Last Plague trilogy**

"So much more than just a horror novel, this one really makes you think. I like books that make me think, and books that present, and pull off, an original idea. This is that book and it's very much a must-read."
**- Castle Macabre**

# CHUMP

Eight stories which take a different look at these reanimated denizens of death:

**CURE WHAT AILS YA -** When a snake oil salesman rolls into the Wild West town of Lobo, both he and the inhabitants are unaware of what is about to crawl out of the desert, hungry for brains.

**1984 -** Finally, after years of being subject to official censure, the true story as to why the Eastern Bloc countries boycotted the 1984 Los Angeles Olympics, is revealed.

**RED SABRE ONE -** An SAS team are tasked with extracting a high value target from their world famous home.

**SENSELESS APPRENTICE -** Step inside the mind of one of the undead, unable to do anything but watch on as his body acts on primal instinct.

**DEAD DROP -** A novella following a courier in the apocalypse. Ceepher's motto is simple; never look inside the package, and always be on time. His latest delivery will put both on the line.

**CHARITY BEGINS AT HOME -** Whilst out collecting for H.O.A.R.D. (Helping Orphans Affected by the Reanimation Disease), Sadie stumbles upon a middle age couple, who seem to have survived the apocalypse with their pristine house intact.

**GONE FISHIN' -** Bored, a son pleads with his dad to tell him, again, how his parents got together...one summers day on the lake.

**WHACKOS -** After 'Reclamation', a radio host and his sound engineer, follow a clean up team, as they confront the after-effects of the zombie apocalypse.